SKELETON MAN

Nonfiction

Seldom Disappointed
Hillerman Country
The Great Taos Bank Robbery
Rio Grande
New Mexico
The Spell of New Mexico
Indian Country
Talking Mysteries (with Ernie Bulous)
Kilroy Was There
The American Detective
**The Best American Detective Stories
of the Century**

SKELETON MAN

TONY HILLERMAN

HarperLargePrint
An Imprint of HarperCollinsPublishers

HarperCollins books may be purchased for educational, business, or sales promotional use. For information, please write: Special Markets Department, HarperCollins Publishers Inc., 10 East 53rd Street, New York, NY 10022.

FIRST HARPER LARGE PRINT EDITION

Printed on acid-free paper

Library of Congress Cataloging-in-Publication Data
Hillerman, Tony.
    Skeleton man / Tony Hillerman.—1st ed.
        p.   cm.
    ISBN 0-06-075423-0 (Large Print)
    ISBN 0-06-056344-3 (alk. paper)
        1. Leaphorn, Joe, Lt. (Fictitious character)—Fiction.
2. Aircraft accidents—Investigation—Fiction. 3. Chee, Jim (Fictitious character)—Fiction. 4. Indian reservation police—Fiction. 5. Police—New Mexico—Fiction. 6. Navajo Indians—Fiction. 7. New Mexico—Fiction. I. Title.

PS3558.I45S47   2004
813'.54—dc22
                                        2004047443

04 05 06 07 08   BVG/RRD   10 9 8 7 6 5 4 3 2 1

This Large Print Book carries the Seal of Approval of N.A.V.H.

While the collision of airliners central to the plot of this book was real and triggered the creation of the Federal Aviation Administration and its flight safety rules, the story and all of its characters are purely fictional. However, several of these fictional folks use names borrowed from generous donors to a fund to assist children stricken with cancer.

The author acknowledges the help of fellow writers Scott Thybony, Michael Ghiglieri, and Brad Dimick—three men who know that great canyon as well as anyone alive—and ethnologist Tandra Love, biologist William Degenhardt, and naturalist Ann Zwinger, whose **Down Canyon** is an American classic. Marty Nelson's research work, as usual, was a huge help.

SKELETON MAN

1

Lieutenant Joe Leaphorn, retired, had been explaining how the complicated happening below the Salt Woman Shrine illustrated his Navajo belief in universal connections. The cause leads to inevitable effect. The entire cosmos being an infinitely complicated machine all working together. His companions, taking their mid-morning coffee break at the Navajo Inn, didn't interrupt him. But they didn't seem impressed.

"I'll admit the half-century gap between the day all those people were killed here and Billy Tuve trying to pawn that diamond for twenty dollars is a problem," Leaphorn said. "But when you really think about it, trace it all back, you see how one thing kept leading to another. The chain's there."

Captain Pinto, who now occupied Joe

Leaphorn's preretirement office in the Navajo Tribal Police Headquarters, put down his cup. He signaled a refill to the waitress who was listening to this conversation, and waited a polite moment for Leaphorn to explain this if he wished. Leaphorn had nothing to add. He just nodded, sort of agreeing with himself.

"Come on, Joe," Pinto said. "I know how that theory works and I buy it. Hard, hot wind blowing gets the birds tired of flying. One too many birds lands on a limb. Limb breaks off, falls into a stream, diverts water flow, undercuts the stream bank, causes a landslide, blocks the stream, floods the valley, changes the flora and that changes the fauna, and the folks who were living off of hunting the deer have to migrate. When you think back you could blame it all on that wind."

Pinto stopped, got polite, attentive silence from his fellow coffee drinkers, and decided to add a footnote.

"However, you have to do a lot of complicated thinking to work in that Joanna Craig woman. Coming all the way out from New York just because a brain-damaged Hopi tries to pawn a valuable diamond for twenty bucks."

Captain Largo, who had driven down from

his Shiprock office to attend a conference on the drunk-driving problem, entered the discussion. "Trouble is, Joe, the time gap is just too big to make you a good case. You say it started when the young man with the camera on the United Airlines plane was sort of like the last bird on Pinto's fictional tree limb, so to speak. He mentioned to the stewardess he'd like to get some shots down into the Grand Canyon when they were flying over it. Isn't that the theory? The stewardess mentions that to the pilot, and so he does a little turn out of the cloud they're flying through, and cuts right through the TWA airplane. That was June 30, 1956. All right. I'll buy that much of it. Passenger asks a favor, pilot grants it. Boom. Everybody dead. End of incident. Then this spring, about five decades later, this Hopi fella, Billy Tuve, shows up in a Gallup pawnshop and tries to pawn a twenty-thousand-dollar diamond for twenty bucks. That touches off another series of events, sort of a whole different business. I say it's not just another chapter, it's like a whole new book. Hell, Tuve hadn't even been born yet when that collision happened. Right? And neither had the Craig woman."

"Right," said Pinto. "You have a huge gap in

that cause-and-effect chain, Joe. And we're just guessing the kid with the camera asked the pilot to turn. Nobody knows why the pilot did that."

Leaphorn sighed. "You're thinking about the gap you see in one single connecting chain. I'm thinking of a bunch of different chains which all seem to get drawn together."

Largo looked skeptical, shook his head, grinned at Leaphorn. "If you had one of your famous maps here, could you chart that out for us?"

"It would look like a spiderweb," Pinto said.

Leaphorn ignored that. "Take Joanna Craig's role in this. The fact she wasn't born yet is part of the connection. The crash killed her daddy. From what Craig said, that caused her mama to become a bitter woman and that caused Craig to be bitter, too. Jim Chee told me she wasn't really after those damned diamonds when she came to the canyon. She just wanted to find them so she could get revenge."

That produced no comment.

"You see how that works," Leaphorn said. "And that's what drew that Bradford Chandler fellow into the case. The skip tracer. He may have been purely after money, but his job was blocking Craig from getting what she was after.

That's what sent him down into the canyon. And Cowboy Dashee was down there doing family duty. For Chee, the pull was friendship. And—" Leaphorn stopped, sentence unfinished.

Pinto chuckled. "Go on, Joe," he said. "How about Bernie Manuelito? What pulled little Bernie into it?"

"It was fun for Bernie," Leaphorn said. "Or love."

"You know," said Largo. "I can't get over our little Bernie. I mean, how she managed to get herself out of that mess without getting killed. And another thing that's hard to figure is how you managed to butt in. You're supposed to be retired."

"Pinto gets the blame for that," Leaphorn said. "Telling me old Shorty McGinnis had died. See? That's another of the chain I was talking about."

"I was just doing you a favor, Joe," Pinto said. "I knew you were getting bored with retirement. Just wanted to give you an excuse to try your hand at detecting again."

"Saved your budget some travel money, too," Leaphorn said, grinning. He was remembering that day, remembering how totally out-it-all he'd felt, how happy he'd been driving north in search of the McGinnis diamond—which he'd never thought had actually existed. Now he was thinking about how a disaster buried under a lifetime of dust had risen again and the divergent emotions it had stirred. Greed, obviously, and hatred, plus family duty, a debt owed to a friend. And perhaps, in Bernie Manuelito's case, even love.

Captain Pinto pushed back his chair, got up.

"Stick around," Leaphorn said. "I want to tell you how this all came out with Bernie and Jim Chee."

"Going to get some doughnuts," Pinto said. "I'll be right back. I want to hear that."

2

As Leaphorn remembered it, the August day he'd been pulled into the Skeleton Man affair had been a total downer moodwise. He'd never felt more absolutely retired in the years he'd been practicing it. The young man across the desk from him, Captain Samuel Pinto, had interrupted jotting something into a notebook when Leaphorn tapped at his door. He'd glanced up with that irritated look interruptions produce, gestured Leaphorn into a chair, put aside the notebook, fished through a stack of folders, pulled two out, and looked at them.

"Ah, yes," said Captain Pinto, "here we are."

Just a few minutes earlier Leaphorn had been hit with the day's first reminder of how unimportant retirees become. At the reception desk below he'd stood, hat in hand, until the young woman in charge looked up from sorting something. He informed her that Captain Pinto was expecting him. She punched a number into the switchboard and glanced up.

"Do you have an appointment?"

Leaphorn had nodded.

She peered at her desk calendar, looked up again at the once-legendary lieutenant, and said, "And you are . . . ?"

A knife-to-the-heart question when delivered in a building where one has worked most of one's adult life, given orders, hired people, and become modestly famous for a mile or two in every direction.

"Joe Leaphorn," Leaphorn said, and saw the name drew not a glimmer of recognition. "I used to work here," he added, but the young lady was already back on the telephone. "Long time ago, I guess," talking to himself.

"The captain said to send you up," she said, and waved him toward the stairway.

Now, in the office marked **Special Investigations**, where Leaphorn used to keep his stuff and do his worrying, Captain Pinto motioned him to a chair.

"I hear Sergeant Chee is finally getting married," Pinto said, without looking up from the paperwork. "What'da you think of that?"

"High time," Leaphorn said. "She's a good girl, Bernie. I think she'll make Chee grow up."

"So we hope," Pinto said, and handed the two folders to Leaphorn. "Take a look at these, Joe. Tell me what you think. Top one's the FBI file on that robbery-homicide down at Zuni. Bunch of jewelry taken and the store operator shot, remember that one? Few days later a Hopi, a fellow named Billy Tuve, tried to pawn an un-set diamond at Gallup. He wanted twenty dollars. Manager saw it was worth thousands. He asked Tuve to stick around while he got an appraisal. Called the police. They took Tuve in. He said an old shaman down in the Grand Canyon gave it to him years ago. Didn't know the shaman's name. McKinley County Sheriff's Office had that jewelry store robbery on its mind. They held him until they could do some checking. Some witnesses they rounded up had reported seeing a Hopi hanging around the jewelry store before the shooting. Then they got an identification on Tuve, found his fingerprints here and there in the store. So they booked him on suspicion."

With all that rattled off, Pinto peered at Leaphorn, awaiting a question. None came. The sound of a Willie Nelson song drifted up from the first floor, a song of lamentation. A piñon jay flew past the window. Beyond the glass Leaphorn saw the landscape that had been his view of the world for half his life. Leaphorn sighed. It all sounded so comfortably familiar. He started reading through the newer folder. On the second page he ran into something that stirred his interest and probably explained why Pinto had wanted to see him. But Leaphorn asked no questions. He'd leave the first questions for Pinto. As a felony committed at Zuni, thus on a federal reservation, this was officially an FBI case. But at the moment it was Pinto's job, doing the legwork, and Leaphorn's old office was now Pinto's office and Leaphorn was merely a summoned visitor.

He finished his study of the new folder, put it carefully on Pinto's desk, and picked up the old one. It was dusty, bedraggled, and very fat.

Pinto waited about five minutes until Leaphorn looked up from his reading and nodded.

"Have you noticed where this Zuni homicide maybe crosses the path of an old burglary case of yours?" Pinto asked. "It's a very cold case out at Short Mountain. You remember it?"

"Sure," Leaphorn said. "But what brought that one out of the icebox?"

"Maybe it's not actually out," Pinto said. "We just wanted to ask you. See if you could think of any connection between this current case here"—Pinto tapped the new folder—"and this old burglary of yours."

Leaphorn chuckled. "You're thinking of Shorty McGinnis's diamond?"

Pinto nodded.

Leaphorn smiled, shook his head, picked up the new file, and opened it. "I must have misread that. I thought the diamond the Hopi fella tried to pawn was valued at . . ." He turned to the second page. "Here it is: 'Current market value of gem estimated at approximately twenty thousand dollars.'"

"That's the figure the appraiser gave the FBI. Said it was three-point-eight carats. The fed jewelry man called it a 'brilliant white with a memory of the sky in it' and said it was 'a special Ascher version of the Emerald Cut,' whatever that means. It's all in that report there."

Leaphorn shook his head again, still grinning. "And mention is made in that new federal file of an expensive unset diamond taken in that old burglary of the Short Mountain Trading Post. I'll bet the FBI man who wrote that is new out here. Can you imagine an expensive diamond at the Short Mountain Trading Post? Or McGinnis actually having one?"

"Well, no," Pinto said. "It would be hard to imagine that. It would strain the mind."

"Anyway, he didn't mention any diamond among the stolen stuff when we investigated that burglary. Maybe he knew I wouldn't believe him. I'm sure you noticed that this note that the diamond should be added to the loot was stuck in the report about a year late. That was after the insurance company complained to the FBI that our burglary report didn't match McGinnis's list of losses."

Pinto was smiling, too. "Maybe he just forgot it. Didn't remember it until he filed his insurance claim."

"Have you asked McGinnis about this?"

"McGinnis is dead," Pinto said. "Long time I think."

Leaphorn sucked in a breath. "Shorty's

dead!" he said. "Be damned. I hadn't heard that."

He rubbed his hand across his forehead, trying to accept it. It was hard to believe that tough, wise, grouchy old man had been just another mortal. And now he had to be added to that growing list of those who had made Leaphorn's past interesting—if not always fun—and left a special vacuum in his life when they died. He looked past Pinto out the window behind him, at the vast blue sky, the thunderhead forming over the Chuskas to the north, remembering sitting with McGinnis in his cluttered trading post, the old man in his rocking chair, sipping whiskey out of an old-fashioned Coca-Cola glass, passing along just as much gossip as he wanted Officer Joe Leaphorn to know and not a word more. Leaphorn looked down at his hands, remembering how McGinnis would hold his glass, tilting it back and forth as he rocked to keep the whiskey from splashing.

"You know," Leaphorn said, and produced a wry chuckle, "I'd forgotten about that burglary."

"I wish the FBI had forgotten it," Pinto said. "Apparently the old man listed the diamond on his insurance claim at ten thousand dollars— which I guess would make it worth twice that these days. And the insurance company complained, objected, and the feds looked into it as maybe a fraud case way back then. And now somebody did a sort of diamond-diamond match in their computer files. It looked strange and they wanted us to check it out."

"Now, doesn't that sound easy? Did they say how to do it?"

"They want to know where that McGinnis diamond came from. Was it recovered? So forth. They seem to have a fairly good witness identification on the Hopi, prints in the store, all that stuff, but the only material evidence is that diamond he was trying to pawn. The theory of the crime seems to be the Hopi took it when he did the Zuni robbery. And it's the only material evidence available so far. So they'd like to know if McGinnis got his diamond back, and did he have one of those jewelry certification forms describing its cut and weight and size and so forth."

Leaphorn nodded.

"So we sent a man out from Tuba City to the store. He said the place had a 'Closed' sign on the door and looked deserted. Said he stopped at a place down the road and they'd heard the old man had a heart attack. Thought he'd been hauled off to Page. Never came back. Checked the hospital. He wasn't there. No record of him. Maybe died in the ambulance or something. Probably his family came and took care of the funeral somewhere."

Leaphorn let that pass without comment. Did Shorty have a family? He couldn't quite imagine that. After a while, Pinto would get to the reason he'd asked Joe to drop in. No hurry. Pinto shuffled some papers, put them back into a folder, looked across the desk at Leaphorn.

"Joe," he said, "did McGinnis tell you where he got that damned diamond? Anything about that?"

"Not a thing. If I had known he'd put it on his insurance claim, I would have asked him. I'd have said, 'Mr. McGinnis, how did you come to have such a fancy diamond?' and McGinnis would have said, 'Officer Leaphorn, that's none of your damned business.'"

Pinto waited for an expansion of that. Leaphorn let him wait. "No ideas, then?"

"Not a one. But now I have a question for you. None of my damned business either, but it seems to me our federal friends are unusually interested in this diamond. I'll bet you noticed that, too, and you asked whichever special agent is dealing with this about it. What did he say?"

Captain Pinto smiled, and it turned into a laugh. "Ah, hell, Joe," he said. "It was George Rice. He said it was just routine, and I said, 'Come on now, Special Agent Rice, you can be honest with me,' and he said, 'Well, you know how it's been since the politicians invented that Homeland Security Agency. They laid a fat new level of political patronage bureaucrats on top of everything we already had to deal with.' Rice said he had a feeling maybe one of the campaign fund-raisers in Washington was doing somebody a favor. You know how it works. Called the regional jefe in Phoenix on the old buddy-buddy basis and told him somebody in the White House would be happy to hear anything we could find out about where this diamond came from. And I told Rice that sounds mysterious, and he said he had the impression it has something to do with a huge estate settlement lawsuit going on back there, and I said that's mysterious, too, and he said it was also a mystery to him, and since it sounded like more Washington politics to him, he'd be happy to keep it that way."

Leaphorn considered this a moment.

"Well," he said, "that makes me sort of glad I'm retired. But why don't you get somebody at work finding McGinnis's family, or whoever

claimed his body. They'd have his stuff, if anything was worth keeping. Maybe that would . . ."
He stopped. Shook his head. "You know, I'm
having trouble believing that old man has left
us."

"They say the good die young. But even men
like Shorty have to go sometime."

"How did it happen?"

"Just natural death. He was old as the mountains, wasn't he?"

Leaphorn sat awhile, staring out the window.
Shook his head. "Hard to believe old Shorty just
died naturally," he said. "Wasn't shot or something."

"Well, we never heard anything to the con-
trary," Pinto said.

Leaphorn got up, recovered his hat.

"Well, I'm sorry I couldn't be more helpful,"
he said. "And if I happen to learn anything about
the McGinnis diamond, I'll let you know. But
I'm not going to lose any sleep over it."

Which, of course, proved to be wrong.

3

The text of the message on Joanna Craig's answering machine didn't seem very important. But the tone of her lawyer's voice told her it was.

"Miss Craig," he had said. "This is Hal Simmons. Our investigators have notified me of something that I should discuss with you. I'll be in my office all afternoon. Please call me when you have time."

She had hardly spoken to Simmons since they'd completed the legal work after her mother's funeral. Now she found his law firm's number in the telephone book, got a busy signal, then called the apartment house doorman and asked him to get her a taxi.

The receptionist at the Simmons law office remembered her from the days when she was there a lot, trying to tie up all those loose ends that death leaves behind even well-organized people. And Joanna Craig's mother was not organized at all. She was erratic, forgetful of things that had happened yesterday, remembering things that had never happened. "Senile dementia," her psychiatrist had called it. Joanna had protested that her mother was too young for senility, and he had said, "Your mother's been through a lot of stress. And her mind has always been— Well, better to say your mother has always had a mind of her own."

However you phrased it, Joanna knew what caused it. It was the death of John Clarke, Joanna's father, and the cruel treatment her mother had received from Clarke's family. Her mother had rarely talked to her about it, and never without crying. But Joanna knew of the injustice. The way her mother had been treated must have been as painful as the loss of her lover. It certainly hurt her daughter.

It wasn't the money, Joanna told herself. She didn't need it. She was getting along fine without it, just as her mother had managed to. It was the cruelty of it. The contempt. That had been a wound that would never heal unless she could finally give her mother justice. And revenge. Maybe what Simmons would tell her would mean that would finally be possible.

He rose from the high-backed chair behind his battered old desk, smiling at her. A big, broad-shouldered man who her mother had told her she could always trust. And she did.

"Miss Craig," he said. "Have a seat. Get comfortable. Explaining this will take a while. I don't want you to expect too much out of what I'm going to tell. But at least it seems to me to represent a chance."

Joanna felt suddenly weak.

"A chance?"

"One of those diamonds seems to have turned up."

She sat down. Closed her eyes.

"Are you all right?" Simmons buzzed his secretary, ordered a glass of water.

"Just the diamonds?" Joanna said, in a voice almost too faint to be heard.

Simmons peered at her. Took the water glass from his secretary and presented it to Joanna, who was looking out the window at the busy streets, at the gray, overcast sky, at the traffic rolling below.

"Remember how your father carried those

diamonds, padlocked to his wrist in that special carrying case your mother told you about? It seems to me that finding them . . ." Simmons paused, looking for a way to put this. "Well, that may finally give us a chance to find his bones. And we've heard a little more about that, too. Just a collection of rumors, perhaps. But . . ."

"Yes," Joanna said. She sat up and straightened her blouse collar. "Tell me everything you've heard. Tell me what you think we should do next."

Simmons tilted back in his chair, took off his glasses, rubbed his eyes, replaced the spectacles, and studied her thoughtfully.

"As friend of your mother, or as lawyer?"

Joanna considered that.

"As lawyer," she said. "Not that you haven't been a good friend."

Simmons sighed. "As friend, I would remind you that you are getting along very well. Good job, and I think the funds your mother left you were always well invested. So you could buy diamonds if you want them and you don't need to make yourself a multi-multimillionaire and start dealing with all the troubles that brings with it. Right?"

"Well, yes," Joanna said. "But that's not the point. It never has been the point."

"I know," Simmons said. "Your mother suffered a lot. And you'd like to see old Plymale pay for that. So would I. But Joann—"

Joanna Craig raised her hand, cut him off. "I'd like to see justice done. I'd like to see him burn in hell."

Simmons considered that a moment, leaned forward.

"Then I'll tell you that if you can find those bones—find anything from which your father's DNA can be extracted—I think we can get your estate claim back into court. With that, and with the evidence in those letters your mother left you, we can establish legally that you are a direct descendant of John Clarke, and thus a direct descendant of Clarke's father. Thereby you can reclaim the Clarke family estate. Thereby you can make Plymale suffer and, from what I've heard of how he has looted that foundation, make him do some burning in bankruptcy court, and probably criminal court as well."

Joanna Craig smiled. "I guess it doesn't sound very Christian. But I'd like that. In fact, I'd enjoy it immensely."

Simmons considered that a moment, shrugged.

"The only way I know of to locate those bones is to find the person who found that container of diamonds. We know it was locked to your father's arm. Trace it back. For the first time that looks faintly possible. And knowing old Plymale, I must warn you that he will be well aware of that possibility. Probably losing sleep thinking about it. Planning what he can do to keep that from happening."

Joanna Craig was still smiling.

"So you are saying go find them?"

"As your lawyer, yes. We'll renew our contract with that investigations agency. I'll keep you informed and advised."

"How about as a friend?"

Hal Simmons shook his head.

"Joanna, as a friend of your mother, as your friend now, I'd say just go home and forget all this. Try to be happy. Even with this diamond showing up, the odds are very slim his body can be found after all these years. And hunting something Plymale doesn't want you to find is sort of like hunting a crocodile in the crocodile's own river."

"Just tell me how to go about it. How to start."

Simmons sighed. "Well, you'll find the man who had the diamond in New Mexico. In the McKinley County jail in Gallup waiting to be indicted for murder. That's where you'll start."

4

Bradford Chandler suddenly swiveled in his beach chair to keep the sea breeze out of his ear. The old bastard had finally said something interesting. Something about diamonds?

Chandler had let his mind wander away from this rambling conversation, just enjoying the feel of the sand blown against the bottom of his bare feet by the Caribbean wind, and the sensation of the sun on his legs, and the sight of the nicely tanned and very shapely girl strolling along the surf line clad in a string bikini and not much else. Thinking of her as prey. Thinking of himself as predator. Enjoying, too, just being here on this very private beach, and his memory of the polished limo pulling up beside the old bastard's private jet with the big black driver holding the door open for him. Savoring the feel of luxury.

Knowing that was the way fate intended it to be for Bradford Chandler. And that was the way it wasn't. Not yet.

"Diamonds?" Chandler said. "You don't expect diamonds in that part of the world. Where did they come from?"

"Mr. Chandler." The old man's tone was impatient now. "You haven't been paying attention. My interest is in one diamond. If I knew where it came from, you wouldn't be sitting in the shade here ogling one of my women."

The old man was Dan Plymale, sitting in a recliner chair and sharing the shade of a huge beach umbrella just to Brad Chandler's left, taking off his sunglasses now and staring at Chandler, his broad, tanned face stern, his hair and his eyebrows dead white, his eyes a pale and icy blue. Reminding Chandler of his deceased father. Bradford Churchill Chandler Sr. Plymale was another of their kind of people. Part of the Anglo-Saxon, Nordic ruling class. Or "we predator people," as his dad would have proudly put it.

Chandler Senior had been deceased nine years now. But, alas, not deceased soon enough. He'd found time to change his will and cut Chandler out of it before he died.

"I just told you I need to know where that diamond came from," Plymale was saying. "I'm ready to talk business now. Are you ready to listen?"

Chandler could not remember anyone ever speaking to him in that tone. He'd overheard it in a hundred luxury hotel lobbies, in the first-class sections of aircraft, and had used it himself sometimes, understanding it reflected the low regard of the luxury class for those below them. But he had never heard it directed at him.

"I was listening," he said. "But you already told me you know where that particular diamond is. It's being held as evidence by the cops in some dinky town in New Mexico. Right?"

"Wrong," Plymale said. "I wasn't asking where it is. I want to know where it came from." Plymale sighed, took a sip from whatever he was drinking. Something iced. Slightly green. Certainly too expensive to be Chandler's normal beverage these days. He loved the taste of such luxury on his tongue.

Plymale moved his bony old man's hand over to a buzzer button on the table between them. Pressed it.

"Bring me another one, and one of whatever my guest is drinking."

Then he leaned back, slipped a folder out of the briefcase on the table, and began leafing through its contents, glancing over at Chandler now and then, sometimes frowning. The drinks arrived on a tray carried by a pretty young woman. No "thank you" came from Plymale, Chandler noticed. He didn't even waste a receptive nod. The very model of Brad Chandler Sr.

"Time for business now. Time to tell you what you need to know. But first we'll give a few minutes to this résumé of yours."

"Résumé?" Chandler said. "I didn't send you—"

"Of course not," Plymale said, looking at Brad quizzically. "That's not the way anyone intelligent collects a résumé. You get it from people who know the subject. People you can trust."

"Oh," said Chandler.

"Like this," Plymale said. "Right here it says—Well, I won't read that. About you getting arrested at a ski resort in Switzerland. Drunk, disorderly, and physical assault on a security type." He looked up from the page, eyebrows raised. "Would you have put that in?"

"No."

"It says, 'Chandler bought out of that.' That right?"

"Right."

"Which Chandler? Is that you or your daddy?"

"Well, I handled it," Chandler said.

"How much did it cost?"

"Let's see. I think it was ten thousand Swiss francs to the guy I hit. And then something to the guy who arranged the payoff."

"Your daddy's money?"

"Sure," Chandler said. He was beginning to resent this.

Plymale switched to another page.

"Bennington," Plymale said. "Three years there. Looks like you made good connections." He read some more. "Looks like some really good connections." He chuckled. "But not good grades. Not wasting your time on the books. The smart boys know why Dad's getting them into those exclusive ruling-class places. Gets 'em connected with the important money. If they like to read books, they can read lots of books later."

"Yeah," Chandler said. Cool now. Smiling at Plymale.

"Didn't work out too well for you, though, did it?"

"Who knows," Chandler said. "It may."

Plymale was on another page now.

"Skippers Incorporated," he said. "Why call it that?"

"They're our business. Hunting down the bail bond skippers, the white-collar thieves. Losers like that. Finding them. Bringing 'em in. Collecting the reward. The bounty."

Plymale indicated what he'd been reading with his finger. "This how you made the connection with Skippers? This affair here where the judge in Portland set your bond at a hundred thousand on that criminal assault charge? Did you skip out on that? It's not clear about that."

"I didn't skip," Chandler said, suddenly nervous and noticing it must have sounded in his voice. He canceled it with a laugh. It was clear enough now, as he'd always suspected, that Plymale hadn't picked him for his good citizenship. He'd been hoping that whoever Plymale had hired to put together this probe into his life wouldn't look too closely into that Portland incident. There was a homicide detective there who had been very interested in that affair. Sort of obsessive, in fact. Kept probing into it. Chandler shook his head. Forget that. But Plymale was staring at him, awaiting an explanation.

"I paid my ten-thousand fee for the bail

bond," he said. "I showed up for trial on time. I got the charges dismissed for lack of evidence. Skippers kept my ten-grand fee and didn't get their bond forfeited. All concerned happy."

Plymale was frowning. "Lack of evidence? It says here the victim suffered broken jaw, broken arm, broken ribs, multiple abrasions. That sounds like a lot of evidence."

"He didn't show up in court."

"Why not?"

Chandler shrugged, glanced at Plymale.

The old man was waiting, wanting an answer.

"I heard his health failed him," Chandler said.

He waited for the next question, staring out at the surf, dealing with the tension. Plymale probably already knew why the bastard hadn't shown up in court. Already knew Chandler was suspected of making sure he couldn't. Making sure the body would never be found. Plymale would ask him, just to see what he'd say. He had an answer ready, but that question didn't come.

"That's when you went to work for Skippers?"

"That's correct," Chandler said, relaxing a little.

"They seem to like the way you go about your job."

"They should. I'm good at it."

"Unusual career, isn't it? I mean for a prep-school boy—Exeter, wasn't it? Who went on to Bennington. Aren't you supposed to get yourself a bride out of the debutante class, a Wall Street job, put on somebody's board of directors? Something that wouldn't involve you in assault charges?"

Chandler produced a yawn, covered it, said, "I guess so." Sounding slightly bored. Feeling the tension easing.

"You like this work?"

"Yep," Chandler said. "Not many dull moments finding these bond skippers. It gives you a chance to exercise your wits. Most of them don't want to be found."

"I noticed that," Plymale said. "I noticed two cases in here involving some shooting."

"Yeah," Chandler said, confident now that this must have been what made him attractive to Plymale. "They shoot and miss, and you shoot and hit," he said. "Otherwise the system isn't efficient."

He glanced at Plymale and found him staring back at him.

"And, both times, the police cleared you."

"Of course," Chandler said. "That's the way it works. You get yourself deputized where you can. Anyway, you're working as a law enforcer, and it's self-defense, and the cops know you just saved them a lot of work and the cost of the trial by shooting the guy. You're doing their job for them. Working off one of their undelivered warrants."

"Well," Plymale said, and put the résumé back into its folder and the folder back into the briefcase. "Time now to tell you what you'd be dealing with here. But first let's enjoy the beach a little. Trot on out there in the surf a ways. Take a few minutes to take a swim and cool off."

Chandler got up, grinning at Plymale. "You'd like me to trot out deep enough to get these swimming trunks soaked, just in case I have one of those high-tech recorder devices wired under them."

Plymale smiled. "Good to be cool, too," he said.

And it was good, Chandler noticed a little later as he sat in his wet trunks listening to Plymale's explanation of the situation. Plymale's law firm, he said, was representing a foundation that was the heir of the Clarke estate. Unfortunately,

Clarke had provided in his will that if his sole offspring survived him, or produced any direct descendants who survived, then he, or they, would inherit instead of the foundation.

"No widow?"

"She was long dead," Plymale said. "And as it happened, this 'sole offspring' was John Clarke. When his daddy heard John was missing in that plane crash, he had a stroke. Died while they were hunting for survivors. No known Clarke offsprings, so our foundation inherited a hell of a lot of wealth. Actually billions, counting real estate and securities."

"Sounds simple enough," Chandler said.

"It was. But it didn't stay simple. A woman turns up, files a civil suit claiming she is the common-law wife of the old man's son, and she's pregnant, and her baby is going to be Clarke's direct descendant. Claims this baby will be old Clarke's grandchild. She wants the fortune for her kid. You with me so far?"

"I think so," Chandler said. "But I don't think I'd want to be her lawyer. And how does this diamond you mentioned come into it?"

Plymale sipped his drink. "If you want to hear this, be patient. Otherwise I call my driver and give you a ride back to my plane. What's your choice?"

"Sorry," Chandler said.

"This woman had a bundle of love letters from Old Man Clarke's kid. The handwriting matched John Clarke's, according to the experts. All are addressed to the claimant. They express joy at their impending marriage, and make some undisguised reference to their previous sexual encounters. In the last of those letters, he says he'll be flying home from Los Angeles the next day and he's bringing her a wonderful diamond engagement ring, and they'll have a fancy wedding. Get married before the kid arrives."

Plymale took another sip.

Chandler raised his eyebrows.

"He knew he had a kid coming, it seems," Plymale said. "He was going to make it legitimate. Luckily for our Plymale law firm, he just waited too long. Then he got on the wrong airplane."

"So they didn't make the fornication legal, did they? Or you wouldn't need me to find that wonderful diamond. Am I right?"

"Partly right. John Clarke got on Trans World Airlines Flight 2 at Los Angeles International

Airport. Flight 2 took off at nine A.M. en route to Kansas City, then on to New York. The potential bride claims that she waited for him at the airport. Waited and waited and waited, with a roomful of other nervous people. Finally, the TWA folks announced the plane was missing. Advised them to leave a telephone number at the desk and go home and wait in comfort. Promised to call when the plane was located."

"Let's see," Chandler said. "Was that about when hijacking airplanes was very popular? Did the plane turn up in Cuba?"

"The crash was in June 1956. Way too early for Castro and all that."

"Oh."

"It was a Lockheed Super Constellation. You old enough to remember them? Four prop engines and a tail with three rudders sticking up. A day later they spotted that funny-looking tail in Arizona, down in the Grand Canyon, and what was left of the cabin upstream a quarter mile or so. And the rest of it scattered here and there up and down the cliffs."

"So you're telling me Clarke was killed then, I guess, but the diamond not found on his body? Is that it? What happened to the Constellation? Struck by lightning or what?"

"Struck by a United Airlines Douglas DC7. That one had left Los Angeles about five minutes earlier, both of them flying at about twenty-one thousand feet, both headed to the East Coast. Storms all around. Nobody knows how it happened, but the investigators guess one of the pilots, maybe both of them, swerved to give the passengers a better look at the canyon. Anyway, a hundred twenty-eight people were killed. Everybody aboard the planes. Worst airline disaster in history up to that time. Bodies scattered up and down the cliffs, all torn up, some of them burned. The planes weren't located until the next day. Then they couldn't get the old-fashioned copters they had then into the canyon due to the canyon winds. Some medics were parachuted down, I'm told, and then they got some mountain climbers to help."

Plymale stopped, peered at Chandler. "You never heard about this?"

"It was old news before I was born."

"Well, back then it was the biggest story of the year." Plymale chuckled. "Quite a show. Not many people flew those days. Took trains. And flying was expensive. One of the planes was mostly hauling serious big shots. A vice president of General Motors, for example, an ex-ambassador, CEO of another Fortune Five Hundred corporation, top level of the social class. Not just the tourist-ticket trash you see now. Very important families involved. One of them even hired some Swiss mountain climbers and had them flown over to see if his daughter's body could be found. A week later they were still hunting pieces of the planes and trying to match body chunks. Hauled them out in bags, in bits and pieces."

Plymale sipped. Chandler waited. Now the old bastard would finally get to the diamond. Probably he wasn't going to ask any more about that homicidal mistake Chandler had made in Portland. Probably it was forgotten now. Even by that homicide detective. A cold, cold case. He sipped his drink. Enjoyed the breeze. Someday he'd be able to afford this lifestyle without putting up with this arrogant treatment.

"Luggage raining down, too," Plymale said. "Suitcases, handbags, those little pet-carrier cages. They found one with a bulldog in it. One with a parrot. Scattering down like a sort of weird hailstorm."

Plymale laughed, enjoying this. "Imagine that. I'd like to have seen it."

"Clarke, too?"

"What?"

"Did John Clarke fall, too?"

"Now, that's a dumb question," Plymale said. "Everybody fell. Pilots, copilots, stewardesses, men, women, children, at least two babies. Some still in the planes, some doing a free fall."

"Did he have the diamond he was bringing for his bride?"

"Probably. He said he was bringing it. He was on the plane when it left LAX. No way to get off." He rattled what was left of the ice in his drink, looked at the glass, shook his head.

The old bastard is teasing me, Chandler thought. To hell with him. To hell with this.

"Look," Chandler said. "I want to know about this job you brought me down here to tell me about. I guess you want me to find something. Maybe John Clarke is still alive. Maybe he didn't get on that plane. Maybe you want me to find what's left of his body if he was on it. Or am I looking for that remarkable diamond he was bringing his lady?"

"You're not very good at guessing," Plymale said. "Nor sitting still and listening."

"Nor playing games, either," Chandler said. "What do you want me to do? And what do I get out of it?"

"I want you to find John Clarke's left arm," Plymale said, and laughed. "How about that? And if you don't find it, I want you to make damn sure nobody else finds it."

Chandler considered this. He glanced at Plymale, who was grinning at him. He finished his drink, put on his sandals, pushed himself out of the chair, and looked down at Plymale.

Plymale's grin went away. "If you walk off now, you'll have been wasting my time and my money," the old man said. "I'll have to find somebody else to do this. You'll be back doing your nickel-and-dime skip-tracing jobs. Chasing after the bond jumpers. And you'll be wondering what you missed."

"Okay," Chandler said. "Then tell me."

"Clarke's left arm seems to have been torn off. The wing of one of those planes cut through the passenger section of the other one. Maybe that did it. Or maybe when he was thrown out of the plane in the collision. Maybe when his body tumbled down a cliff." Plymale shrugged. "Doesn't matter how. What matters is that it was his left arm, because Clarke had one of those security cases attached to his left wrist. Handcuffed, sort of. Like the devices State Department couriers used to carry secret stuff. Jewelry dealers and some big-currency brokers used to use 'em, too. Lock them on, lock the case, nobody would have the second key but the person who was getting the delivery."

"Sure," Chandler said.

"Anyway, sometime after the disaster, a fellow working at the canyon bottom saw part of the arm—hand, wrist, forearm, pretty much all of it, I think it was. It was sticking out of a pile of driftwood and trash at one of those Colorado River waterfalls. He saw the forearm with the handcuff on it and the box attached to a chain. He even saw a tattoo on the bicep. Claimed he did, anyway. But he couldn't get to it. Went back to the place the next day with some help, but the river had risen and swept away the flotsam. And the arm with it, or so we presume. Who knows? Could be somebody else came along and fished it out."

"And got the diamond case?"

Plymale shook his head. "Maybe. Anyway, that's the end of that phase of the story."

"Why the security case?" Chandler asked. "He could have carried that diamond ring for his bride in his pocket."

"Clarke was managing part of his old man's jewelry business. He'd gone to the coast to bring back a shipment of 'special-cut' diamonds for the rich end of his trade. They were the very best, blue-white, perfect gems, specially cut for the cream of the elite. I think there was seventy-something of them listed in the claim, all at least two and a half carats. The airline insurance company paid its hundred-thousand maximum limit for the loss. People in the business guess they'd have been worth a hundred times that, even at prices then. Today, who knows. Smallest one would probably sell for more than twenty thousand. Say double that for an average, and then multiply it by about seventy-five. Many multiple millions."

Chandler was no longer bored. Or tired.

"And they were never recovered?"

"Not legally, anyway. Not reported and returned to owner. That's the problem," Plymale said. "Maybe they have been. Maybe we're trying to find who has them now."

That didn't make sense to Chandler. This old man was not going to be somebody he could trust, he thought. Ironic, he thought. Neither was he.

"It seems to me if somebody had found them, they'd have been cashed in by now," Chandler said. "Don't you think?"

"If they had been put on the market, we'd know about it. The Clarke family and the insurance company had the alert out to jewelry dealers. Here and in Europe and everywhere else. The DeBeers monopoly keeps an eye out, too, and those stones were rare enough at their price and that special cut so they'd have been noticed. And they haven't been," Plymale said.

He checked his empty glass, put it down, looked at Chandler. "Not until this one showed up in that robbery in New Mexico."

"Oh? You going to tell me about that? Now we're getting to the bottom line." Chandler had been imagining finding that jewel container. Leather maybe, or some tough plastic. Zipper would be locked. He'd cut it open. Pour them out into his palm. One by one. Examine them. Estimate their worth.

"Arm hasn't been found, either," Plymale said.

Chandler laughed. "Who cares about that damned arm?"

"I do. A lot. And I think you will, too, if you want this job," Plymale said. He studied Chandler, waiting for Chandler to ask him why.

"Why?"

"Those diamonds are just a chance to make

some walking-around money on the side," Plymale said. "Just peanuts. But the arm is what's important."

Chandler's expression was puzzled. No need to fake it.

"This woman Clarke was coming home to marry, her daughter is into that psychic stuff. Or claims she is. Crystal gazing, pyramid power, all that flaky stuff. At least that's what we hear. Her name's Joanna Craig. Lives in New York. She's been running some little ads out in Grand Canyon country, spreading the word among National Park guides, tour directors, so forth, that there's a hundred-thousand-dollar reward for that arm."

"Well, now," Chandler said. "Do you know why?"

"We are told that she claims she has received a psychic message from young Clarke from beyond the grave. In this dream she claims this Clarke ghost tells her his missing arm is hurting him. He tells her she's his daughter and she must find that arm of his and get it buried with the rest of him."

Chandler noticed he was smiling.

"That's her story," Plymale said. "Trouble is most of those bodies were so torn up that they couldn't be collected and put back together. Some burned to ashes, some eaten by the coyotes before they were found, a lot of the bits and pieces buried together in common graves. How would you like to go into court with that sort of evidence?"

Chandler grinned. "So we dig us up another set of left-arm bones and collect the reward. But I bet you already thought of that."

"Of course," Plymale said. "You're not as slow as you've been acting. Of course, it wouldn't work. According to the ad she ran, he had a fracture of that forearm set a few years earlier. X-rays and so forth. Had to be pinned together. You couldn't get away with it."

"Oh, well," Chandler said, thinking of the diamonds again. "Just tell me what you're after. And what you want me to do. And what's in it for Bradford Chandler."

"Were you paying attention when I mentioned that civil law suit? Well, pay attention now. This gets complicated. Old Man Clarke was a widower. No near kin except his son, John. In the suit Joanna's mother filed way back then, she claimed this Joanna was the baby John Clarke got her pregnant with. That makes Joanna Craig a granddaughter of John Clarke's daddy. That makes her the 'direct descendant' who inherits the family fortune."

Chandler looked at Plymale, said, "Light begins to dawn. Need I ask who has all that Clarke fortune now?"

"The way the will was written, if there weren't any of those direct descendants, then the money went to this nonprofit charity foundation we helped him set up. I think I explained that."

"Ah," Chandler said. "And you were the executor of his estate?"

Plymale ignored the question. "Joanna Craig's mother-to-be got herself a lawyer, but the only evidence she had was a bundle of old letters. It was too weak to back up a court claim. We tried to make a settlement with her. She turned that down and that looked like the end of it."

"She sounds crazy," Chandler said.

"She was crazy. Old Man Clarke said she was schizophrenic-paranoid. Seemed sane enough when she was taking whatever medicine the shrinks give 'em for that. But crazy, anyway."

Plymale paused, signaled for another drink. Waited. Chandler looked out across the beach at the surf coming in, at the girl in the string bikini, who was coming back now, accompanied by another bikini-clad girl. They were looking his way, laughing.

The drink arrived. Plymale took a sip. Poked Chandler's arm. "Pay attention now," he said. "Here's why we give a damn about finding that arm. Those damned scientists now claim they can recover DNA evidence from old bones. Even awful old bones, like in the Egyptian pyramids. You know what that means?"

Chandler nodded, but Plymale told him anyway. It meant that John Clarke's lost left-arm bones with the old fracture x-rays and maybe even with the diamond case still handcuffed to the wrist could prove that Joanna Craig actually was the man's daughter.

And, Chandler was thinking, that would mean that old man Plymale would lose control of a huge amount of money. Maybe there would be an outcome even worse than that for Plymale. The court might order Plymale to account for what his "nonprofit charity" had been doing with that mountain of money all the years he had controlled it.

Chandler was staring at the two girls in the bikinis, but his mind was focused on that mountain of wealth.

5

Within minutes after getting home from his meeting with Pinto, Leaphorn knew this worrying about diamonds wouldn't just go away. The light on his answering machine was blinking and the second call was from Deputy Sheriff Cowboy Dashee. With a diamond on his mind.

The first one was from Professor Louisa Bourbonette, sounding happy. The old woman she'd gone to see at Bitter Springs had been a treasury of Havasupai legendary stuff. Tomorrow the old lady would take Louisa to see an even more elderly uncle who was full of lore about the Paiute people.

"I'm going to stay down here tonight. Tomorrow I'll find this fellow and see what I can get on tape. I'll call you again tomorrow and let you know when to expect me. I think it's going to link the Havasupai origin story with the Hopi's. Wish you were down here with me. You'd be interested in these legends. And don't forget tomorrow is garbage pickup day on your street."

Joe hadn't forgotten. He'd already wheeled the can out to the curb for the Window Rock Trash Co. truck.

The second call was the sort that retired people learn to expect.

"Lieutenant," Dashee said, "two of your former hired hands have set themselves a getting-married date. It's going to be two weeks from Monday, at Bernie Manuelito's mother's place, south of Shiprock. You're invited. I get to be best man. In case you haven't guessed, Bernie's chosen one is finally, at long last, Jim Chee."

Then came Cowboy Dashee's chuckle, followed by a short pause, and then it was time for what retired people know follows friendly introductory statements:

"And, Lieutenant, I've got a problem. Like to talk to you about it. Maybe get some advice. This man they're holding in that Zuni robbery-homicide thing, well, he's my cousin. That diamond he was trying to pawn, well, he says he's had that thing for years. He didn't do that robbery. I'd like to get your help on that."

Dashee paused. He cleared his throat. Leaphorn sighed.

"Ah," said Dashee, "Sergeant Chee suggested I ask you about this. Get some advice. He told me something about that old trading post operator way up there at Short Mountain, between Tuba City and Page—McGinnis, I think it is. Anyway, Chee said that in one of your old burglary cases, McGinnis reported having a big diamond stolen from his store. Could you let me know if you have any time to fill me in on that?" Another pause. "Well, thank you, sir."

Did he have any time? Did he have anything else? Leaphorn dialed the number Dashee left, got Dashee's answering machine, left a message saying he had time. Plenty of time. Nothing but time. Besides, this diamond thing was different enough to be interesting. He looked in the refrigerator, saw nothing appealing, put on his hat, and went out to his pickup. He'd get a sandwich down at the Navajo Inn and then he'd— He'd what? Watch people playing golf on afternoon television? Play the Free Cell solitary game on the computer? Listen to all those lonely little sounds a house makes when it's empty? To hell with that. He dialed the Dashee number again.

"Turns out I'll be going over into your terri-
tory today," he told the answering machine. "I'll
stop at the Hopi Cultural Center for some late
lunch. You could meet me there if it's handy.
Otherwise, I'm going on to that old Short
Mountain Trading Post. Maybe you could catch
me there."

That done, he wrote a note to Louisa telling
her he was taking care of business north of
Tuba City and would call her. He climbed into
his truck, thinking about Sergeant Chee finally
getting wise enough to realize that Bernie loved
him. That led him to consider whether he
should, once again, suggest to Professor Louisa
Bourbonette that they get married. He'd proposed that once, when they decided she would
use his Window Rock house as the northern base
of her endless research on the mythology of
Navajo, Ute, Paiute, Zuni, Hopi, and any other
tribes she could persuade to talk into her tape
recorder. The first time he'd asked her, the answer had been brief and determined.

"Joe," she had said, "I tried that once and I
didn't like it."

The next time he brought it up, she reminded him that he was still in love with Emma,

which was still true even though ten years had passed since Emma had left him a lonely widower. Louisa said she would give him another ten years to think about it.

Leaphorn sighed, decided to leave well enough alone again, and made the westward turn onto U.S. 264. He paused at Ganado to top off his gas tank, and spent the next hour trying to decide how to tell Dashee he had not the slightest idea what he could do to help his cousin. No profit in that thought. He shifted to trying to restore his usual Navajo harmony with the world around him—a world in which too many of his old friends seemed to be dying. Even Shorty McGinnis, hard as that was for him to realize.

The Bureau of Land Management pickup he'd last seen Dashee driving wasn't among the four vehicles in the Hopi Cultural Center parking lot, a disappointment. But the pretty Hopi receptionist in the center's café recognized him (the first bright spot in the day) and gave him a huge smile. Of course she knew Dashee. He hadn't been in, but she'd tell him Lieutenant Leaphorn had been there and was driving on to Short Mountain. Leaphorn drank two cups of coffee, ate the Hopi cook's version of the taco, and headed for Tuba City and the great emptiness of the multicolored cliffs and canyons that lay beyond it.

He paused in Tuba looking for friends he'd made there a lifetime ago as a green rookie cop. It would be good, he thought, to catch them before they cashed in and went off on that Last Great Adventure with the Holy People. He found three, one too busy to do much visiting, one nursing a bad bout with arthritis, and his former Tuba City district sergeant, who was all too happy to remind him of the mistakes he used to make. That took time.

He headed north out of Tuba City, driving faster than he should, but when he made the left turn onto the washboard gravel of Navajo Route 6130, the westering sun was low enough to be blinding.

That discomfort was more than offset in the eyes of Leaphorn (with his Navajo conditioning to apply value to beauty, and economic importance to the weather) by the great ranks of towering clouds rising like white castles to the north and west. The usual late-summer "monsoon" was late. Maybe much-needed rain was finally arriving.

He bumped across Big Dry Wash (the sometimes site of roaring runoff floods) and over the ridge into Bikahatsu Wash and onto the Blue Moon Bench.

There the only buildings were the Short Mountain Trading Post, a big slab-sided barn with its pole-fenced pen for sheep connected to a smaller one for other animals, and the store itself, with two gasoline pumps standing beside it. The only vehicle in the packed earth of the parking space was a rusty and windowless old Ford sedan. Its wheels were missing. It rested on blocks with a collection of tumbleweeds trapped beneath it.

Leaphorn parked beside it, turned off his ignition, and sat studying the scene, checking it against his memories, looking with fading hopes for some sign of life. The long wooden bench was still on the porch, but the customers who sat there exchanging gossip and drinking the cold soda pop McGinnis provided them were absent. The livestock pens were empty. If any hay bales were stacked in the barn, he couldn't see them. And except for a mild breeze, now pushing a tumbleweed along to add to the old car's collection, the silence was absolute.

Leaphorn glanced at his watch. Plenty of time had passed for McGinnis to have opened the door, peered out, and waved him in. But the door hadn't opened. Now he was forced to face what Captain Pinto had told him. John McGinnis had died, was dead, gone forever, Pinto had it right. Leaphorn had simply doubted because he hadn't wanted to believe. He faced it now, admitted to himself that he had made this long drive hoping to find that Pinto was wrong, or someone to tell him how it had happened. Somebody said it was a heart attack. More likely a stroke. McGinnis would never have gone to a hospital willingly to die among strangers. Leaphorn had expected to find someone here to reassure him about that. Someone with whom he could trade memories. But he'd found only empty, dusty silence.

He got out of the truck, trying to decide what to do, thought of nothing useful, and let habit guide him. He mounted the steps to the porch floor and knocked, and knocked again. No answer. None expected. The sign was still beside the door, telling all who came: THIS ESTABLISHMENT FOR SALE INQUIRE WITHIN. Had a new owner bought it? Highly unlikely. Leaphorn knocked again. No response. He walked down the porch to the nearest window, brushed away the dust, put his forehead against the glass, shaded his eyes, and looked in.

Rows of mostly empty shelves, the old man's desk at the end of a long counter, to Leaphorn's right, a blinking light. A blinking light? He focused on it through the dirty glass. A television set showing what seemed to be a beer commercial in black and white. In front of the set, the back of what seemed to be a rocking chair, and the back of the head of someone sitting in the chair. White hair.

Leaphorn sucked in a deep breath, went back to the door, knocked again, and tried the door handle. Unlocked. He pulled the door open and stood staring into the room.

"Mr. McGinnis," he shouted. "Shorty?" And he hurried in.

It was McGinnis and he was alive, but Leaphorn wasn't sure of that until he was almost close enough to touch him. Then McGinnis lifted his left hand to adjust the gadget that was holding an audio device over his ears. While doing that he noticed Leaphorn and turned in the rocking chair.

"You born in a barn?" McGinnis asked. "Nobody ever teach you about knocking before you come walking right in?"

Leaphorn found himself not knowing what to say. He watched McGinnis pushing himself awkwardly out of the rocking chair and taking off the earphones he'd been using.

"Back in Window Rock they think you're dead," Leaphorn said. "That's what I was told."

"Speak up," McGinnis said. "My hearing ain't what it was, and I can't make it out when you're mumbling. But I'm supposed to be dead, huh?"

"Dead and gone."

McGinnis had put on his spectacles and was leaning on the back of his chair, peering at Leaphorn.

"Let's see now," he said. "You're that Navajo policeman. Used to come out here years ago and drink my soda pop and get me to tell you where to find people. That right? You were out here a lot when Old Man Tso got murdered, I remember that. And I believe your granddaddy was that old fella they called Horse Kicker. Am I right? And your mother was a Gorman. One of the Slow Talking Dinee."

"My grandfather was Hosteen Klee, and nobody ever called him Horse Kicker but you," Leaphorn said. "And Mr. McGinnis, I want to say I'm glad they're wrong about you being dead."

"If you thought I was dead, what the devil brought you way out here? What are you after? You don't come here not wanting something."

Before Leaphorn could answer, McGinnis was hobbling back through the store toward the doorway that led to his living quarters.

"I'm going to make you some coffee," he said. "Unless you broke that habit you had of not drinking whiskey."

"I'll take coffee," said Leaphorn, following McGinnis. But he grimaced as he said it. After all these years he could still remember the awful acidic flavor of the old man's brew.

McGinnis lit the propane stove on what passed as his kitchen work space, took a chipped cup and a Coca-Cola glass out of the cabinet above. He put his coffeepot over the burner and took a bottle of Jack Daniel's out of a drawer. He opened that and carefully poured until the glass was filled up to the bottom of the red trademark **C**.

"Have a seat," he said. "I'll take a sip or two

of this while your coffee gets made and you can tell me what you want me to do for you. Tell me what sort of favor you're after this time."

"Well, first I want to know how you're doing. Looks like you're still in business. Still grouchy as ever."

McGinnis snorted, sipped his bourbon, sipped again. He held the glass up close to his eyes, studied it, picked up the bourbon bottle, and dribbled in enough to restore the liquid level up to the bottom of the **C**.

"Business?" he said. "Just barely. Customers all starved out, or they drive over to Page and do their buying there. Once in a while somebody comes in. Usually it's just to offer to trade me something. That's sort of what I'm doing now. Just getting rid of what I've got left. The giant oil company folks, they already quit bringing the gasoline supply truck out here. Said I didn't buy as much as they burned driving the delivery truck out."

They talked awhile about that, about how Old Lady Nez came by with her daughter every once in a while and baked him some bread and did some other cooking for him in exchange for some of the canned goods he still had on his shelves.

"Except for that, I don't see many people anymore. And now we've got that covered, you're going to ask me what you want to know."

"All right," Leaphorn said. "I want to know about that robbery you had."

"Wasn't a robbery. Robbery they point a gun at you and take your stuff. Cop like you ought to know the difference. This was a burglary. Broke in after I was sleeping, took a box of canned meat, sugar, stuff like that, and the money I had in my cash box. Mostly food, though. That what you want to know? I can't tell you much. It didn't wake me up."

He gave Leaphorn a slightly sheepish smile and held up the bourbon bottle.

"I'd been watching that damned TV set and sipping a little more than I should. Didn't even hear the son of a bitch. Didn't know he'd been there until I noticed stuff gone from the grocery shelves."

"Just grocery? They take anything else?"

"Took the blanket I had hanging on a rack in there, and some ketchup, and . . ." he frowned, straining to remember. "I believe I was missing a box of thirty-thirty ammunition. But mostly food."

"None of it ever recovered?"

McGinnis laughed. "'Course not," he said. "If the burglar didn't eat it, you cops would have done that if you caught him."

"You didn't mention a diamond. How about that?"

"Diamond?"

"Diamond worth about ten thousand dollars."

McGinnis frowned. Took another tiny sip. Looked up at Leaphorn.

"Oh," McGinnis said. "That diamond."

"The one you mentioned on the insurance claim report. You listed it as a ten-thousand-dollar diamond."

"Oh, yeah," McGinnis said, and took another sip of his bourbon.

"Did you get it back?"

"No."

"Did you get your insurance money for it?"

McGinnis peered at Leaphorn, blinked his watery blue eyes, rubbed his hands across them, put down his glass, and sighed.

"I remember that time, years ago, you came in here trying to find a shaman. Margaret Cigaret, I believe it was—a Listener, as I recall her. And I told you who her clan was, and about a Kinaalda being held for one of the little girls in her clan, and you was smart enough to know Old Woman Cigaret would likely be out where they was holding that ceremonial and we sort of got acquainted."

Having finished that statement to remind Leaphorn of his good deed, McGinnis nodded, signaling Leaphorn that he could comment on his helpfulness without violating the polite Navajo ban against interrupting.

"I remember," Leaphorn said. "You also told me you knew my grandfather. You claimed they used to call Hosteen Klee Horse Kicker. It made my mother mad at you when I told her that. She said only a liar would say something like that."

"Boys shouldn't tell their mothers such things. Insulting your grandfather," McGinnis said, choosing to ignore the implication. "Anyway, that day it got to be more like two friends talking. You and me. Not like you was a lawman." He peered at Leaphorn, quizzically.

Leaphorn nodded.

"You still thinking that way?"

Leaphorn considered that. "When Captain Pinto told me you died, that didn't seem right to me. I didn't want to believe it. Too many old friends are dying. I didn't really think I could learn anything about that diamond out here. I just wanted to see if I could bring back some old memories about when I was really a policeman. Maybe it would help me get into harmony with living with so many of my friends gone."

McGinnis picked up his glass, made a sort of semi-toasting gesture with it and took a sip, hoisted himself from the rocker, and shuffled off through the doorway into his bedroom.

Leaphorn sipped his coffee. His memory of the chemical taste proved accurate. He put down the cup, grimaced, watched the dust float through the shaft of sunlight slanting through the window, remembering how this place (and his own life) had been when he'd been a young cop working out of Tuba City, learning the trade.

McGinnis emerged, lowered himself into the rocker, put the pouch on his lap, and looked at Leaphorn, expression stern.

"Now it's time for you to tell me what kind of information you want to get from me."

"Fair enough," Leaphorn said. "You may have read about that robbery at Zuni a while back. It was in the papers. On TV. On the radio."

"Fella killed one of them tourist-trap operators, wasn't it?" McGinnis said. "One of those places where tourists buy all that Indian junk. Heard it on the radio. Fella got off with some money and a bunch of other stuff."

"Right," Leaphorn said. "Well, now they have a suspect in jail at Gallup. A Hopi who tried to pawn a diamond worth maybe twenty thousand and he wanted only twenty dollars in pawn. FBI thinks he must have gotten it in the robbery. But he claims a man gave it to him down in the Grand Canyon years ago. This Hopi's name is Billy Tuve and he's a cousin of Cowboy Dashee. You remember Cowboy?"

McGinnis nodded.

"Dashee says Tuve's not guilty. Captain Pinto saw the reference to the diamond in that insurance stuff added to your burglary. Diamonds aren't common out here. So I wondered if you knew anything useful."

"Well, then," McGinnis said. "That's interesting. This Tuve, he claims he got it from a man down in the bottom of Grand Canyon, did he?"

He hoisted himself out of the rocker, shuffled down the store's aisle, and disappeared again through the doorway into the living quarters.

Leaphorn sat thinking his thoughts. How much the man had aged. How McGinnis and his store seemed to be dying together. He resumed his study of the dust particles drifting through a beam of light from the lowering sun.

McGinnis came down the aisle with a small pouch of what seemed to be deer skin hanging from his right hand. He reseated himself in the rocker, looked at Leaphorn.

"I'll tell you a story. You decide if it helps any. Probably won't."

Leaphorn nodded.

"Years ago. Winter, I remember. One of the cold ones. Lots of snow. A fellow came in here, said his name was Reno, probably middle thirties, riding a horse and all bundled up. Wearing a felt hat tied on with a strip of blanket holding the brim down over his ears. He said he needed some food and to use my telephone. My line was down, so I told him he could get to one at that store at Bitter Springs, and if that one wasn't working, he'd have to get all the way to Page. He got some stuff off the shelf and I heated up a can of pork and beans for him. Then he said he didn't have any money but he would leave me his horse and saddle for some more food and for me giving him a ride into Page."

McGinnis chuckled at the memory, located his Coca-Cola glass, poured a trickle of bourbon into it, took a sip, and shook his head.

"It was a little roan mare and pretty used up. Limping on its back leg. Fairly good saddle, though. I put the horse in the barn with some hay, thinking I wasn't going to make anything out of the deal, but if I didn't take the horse, I'd probably be stuck with the cowboy, too. I asked him where he was coming from. And now we come to the funny part. He said he been down in the canyon with a bunch of hippies and got lost from that crowd and was trying to find a way out of there. Said he ran into an old Indian while he was trying to climb up a side canyon. The old man told him that slot he was going up was a dead end, and showed him how to get to a trail the horse could manage, and asked him if he had a good knife or a hatchet he'd be willing to part with. So Reno said he showed the fella his knife and said he'd take ten dollars for it. The Indian didn't have any money but he offered a trade."

Having said that, McGinnis took another sip, picked the leather pouch off his lap, and started trying to untie the thong that held it closed.

McGinnis looked up from his labor. "You've seen 'em like this afore," he said.

"Looks like a pouch to hold his ceremonial pollen," Leaphorn said. "Or carry the cornmeal to use for a blessing. But I don't recognize that figure stitched into the leather. It looks a little like a baseball umpire with his chest protector. What kind of Indian was he? Hopi? Havasupai? Hualapai? Yuman? Could even be one of the Apache tribes. They all use medicine pouches."

"This cowboy, this Reno, said he didn't know much about Indians. But he said this old fellow talked a lot about Masaw, or however you pronounce that kachina. Anyway, the Hopis know about him, and I think some of the Yuman people down in the canyon, too. And the Supai folks. Some of them call him Skeleton Man. Supposed to be the Guardian of the Underworld, and the spirit who greeted the first Hopis when they came up from the dark world they been living in. This spirit told them how to make their religious migrations and where to live when they finished doing that. And the big thing about him for the Hopis, this spirit taught them not to be afraid of death."

McGinnis paused, took another sip.

"Getting hoarse," he said. "That's the most I've talked in a while. But anyway, he's supposed to have let a bunch of Hopi elders look down into the underground and see where people who died were living comfortable and having a good time."

McGinnis stopped, examined the whiskey level in his glass. "What was that you asked me about?"

"What was in the little pouch?"

"Well, it wasn't pollen. There was nothing blessed in this medicine pouch," McGinnis said. He poured the contents out into his palm.

A small round metal box emerged, worn-looking and with the legend **Truly Sweet** in red on its side. A snuff box, Leaphorn thought. Not much of that used on the reservation these days.

McGinnis twisted off the lid and extracted a clear blue-white stone, marble-sized but not marble shape. He held it out between thumb and forefinger, rotating it in a beam of sunlight. The sunlight flashed through it, touching off glittering bursts of light.

"When you pour your pollen out of your pouch," McGinnis said, "then you're pouring out a blessing. That's the symbol of regerminating life. Of everything good and healthy and natural. Pour this little bastard out and you got the symbol of greed. It's the sign of what folks cheat and steal and kill for. White women like to wear them to show other folks how rich they are."

He held it out in a beam of sunlight, admired it. "Pretty, ain't it?"

"Ah," Leaphorn said, and smiled. "Mr. McGinnis, you're starting to sound like an old-fashioned traditional Navajo."

"Not quite," McGinnis said. "But remember, when that First Man spirit fella of yours, when he was talking about the witchcraft evil stuff he had in his medicine bundle, he called it 'the way to make money.' Always did think that was a good point we whites overlooked. I mean, when a fella had more stuff than he needed and was stacking more of it up with the people all around him hungry, that was a pretty good clue he had some of that greed sickness, and they collect these things to prove they're better at being greedy than their friends."

With that, McGinnis produced a creaky old man's chuckle and put the diamond back into the tin and the tin into the medicine pouch.

"Somebody said money was the root of all evil," McGinnis said. "Myself, I never did well enough here to get much of it."

"How about the diamond? Sounds like you wanted to make that work for you."

McGinnis reached out and dropped the pouch into Leaphorn's hand, changing the subject. "Take another look at it. Up close. It's pretty, all right. But nothing to go to jail for."

Leaphorn extracted the snuff can from the pouch, took out the diamond, and let the sunlight shine through it. He turned it, examined it.

"Seems to have been shaped to fit into some sort of necklace. A pendant. You just gave him some groceries for it and got you his horse, too? I'd say you struck a pretty hard bargain," he said. "Sounds to me like you were trying to practice 'the way to make money.'"

McGinnis looked defensive. "You're making it sound worse than it was. My pickup was still running then. I gave him a ride into Page. Figured it was a fake, anyway. So did Reno."

Leaphorn looked surprised. "Well, now. Is that right? Then how come you estimated it at ten thousand dollars when that burglar stole it?"

McGinnis laughed, peered at Leaphorn, raised his eyebrows. "Are we still having a friendly conversation here? Or are you back to being a cop?"

"Let's keep it friendly."

"Well, then. I told this young fella I wasn't born yesterday and I knew all about those artificial diamonds. Zircons, I think they are. Did he really think I'd believe he was giving me a genuine diamond for a little food and a ride through the snowstorm? And he said, to tell the truth, he'd have been disappointed in me if I did. He said he always figured it was artificial."

"You say he admitted it was a fake?"

McGinnis nodded. "Yeah. Reno said he figured that old fellow who gave it to him was either sort of crazy or a religious nut. Thought he might be trying to organize some sort of cult to the Skeleton Man down there."

"But you listed it as an expensive diamond in the burglary report. If I hadn't known you so long, that would surprise me."

"Well, after the burglary I got to thinking about it, and I thought maybe I was just getting too cynical about things. Probably it really was a real diamond." McGinnis peered at Leaphorn, nodded. "Yes," he said. "A real perfect stone, too."

"What's the rest of the story?" Leaphorn asked. "You found it again after you filed the burglary report? Or the burglar really took it but brought it back?"

"Take your pick," McGinnis said. "The insurance company cut my claim way down, anyway."

"How about an address for this Reno?"

McGinnis laughed. "I said, 'Where you from, son?' and he said, 'Reno. That's why they call me that.'"

Leaphorn examined the stone again. "I've seen zircon stones. This looks like a diamond."

"I think it is," McGinnis said. "This cowboy, or whatever he was, said, 'How could an old Indian down in the canyon get one of those?' Laughed at the idea." He pointed to the pouch in Leaphorn's hand.

"Take a look at that, Joe," he said. "I guess that's some sort of lizard stitched there into the leather. But I never saw one like it. And that fierce-looking insect on the other side—you reckon that's got something to do with that fella's religion?"

"I'll show it to Louisa," Leaphorn said. "She's down in the canyon now collecting oral-history stuff from the Havasupai people down there."

"Keep it, then," McGinnis said. "You want to hear the story he told me?"

"I think that's what I came for," Leaphorn said. "Remember, Cowboy Dashee's cousin claims he got his diamond from an old man down in the canyon."

"I already told you some of this," McGinnis said.

"I'd like to hear it again. See if you tell it the same."

McGinnis nodded. "Maybe I left something out. Well, anyway, this Reno says it was raining and sleeting and he was leading his horse up one of those narrow slots runoff waters cut in the canyon cliffs, thinking maybe he could follow it all the way out to the surface. Up there a little ways he passed the mouth of one of those washes that drains into the canyon, and this old man was standing in it out of the weather. My cowboy rolls himself a cigarette, and one for the old man. The old man asks if he's got a knife or a hatchet he'd be willing to swap for something. Reno shows him one of those big folding knives he was carrying in one of those belt holsters. The old man admires it. He goes back into his cave, and when he comes out again, he has a sort of fancy flat box. Looked like one a peddler might carry and it has a whole bunch of little snuff cans in it. He opens one of them and takes out a little gem and holds it out like he's offering it to swap. Reno says no. The old man gets out a bigger one. Then Reno says he decided it might be worth as much as his old knife, and his girlfriend would go for that. So he makes the trade."

McGinnis shrugged, took another sip.

"That's it?"

"End of story," McGinnis said.

"This Reno saw several diamonds in that box?"

McGinnis pondered. "I guess so. Actually, I think he saw several of those little cans. He said something about a bunch of those little snuff cans. He said he guessed the old man used them to keep the diamonds safe."

"Where did this fancy box come from?"

"Reno said he asked the old man that. The Indian fellow couldn't speak English but he made airplane gestures, and sort of simulated a plane crash and everything falling down. And then a big fire."

Leaphorn considered this, with McGinnis watching.

"Mr. McGinnis," Leaphorn said. "Were you living here in, let's see, 1956 I think it was?"

McGinnis laughed. "I was waiting to see if you're still as smart as you used to be," he said. "You passed the test. It was summer, June, before the rains start. Up to then, it was the worst airline disaster in history. Couple of those big airlines collided."

"And it happened just about there," Leaphorn said, pointing out the window toward the rim of Marble Canyon—not visible from here but no more than twenty miles away.

McGinnis was grinning. "I got a bunch of clippings about that back with my stuff," he said. "It was old news by the time I got out here, but people still talked about it. Two of the biggest airlines of the time ran together, tore the end off of one of them and the wing off the other one, and everything was all torn up and falling into the canyon. Bodies of a hundred and twenty-eight people showering down the cliffs. Most exciting thing that ever happened around here."

"And all their luggage, too," Leaphorn said.

"And you're thinking that might have included a leather-covered peddler's case with a lot of jewelry in it."

"That's exactly what I'm thinking," Leaphorn said.

"Tell the truth, that same thought did occur to me, too," McGinnis said. "And I didn't think a jewelry drummer would be carrying zircons in such a fancy case."

6

Almost everyone liked Bernadette Manuelito. Always had. Her teammates on the Shiprock High girls' basketball team liked her. She was popular with her fellow botany students when she worked as an assistant in the university biology lab. Other recruits in the Navajo Police Department training program approved of her— and so did those she worked with during her short stint with the U.S. Border Patrol. Ask any of them why and they'd tell you Bernie was always cheerful, happy, laughing, brimming with good nature.

But not today.

Today, as she drove her old blue Toyota pickup west on U.S. 64 toward Shiprock en route to a dutiful call upon Hosteen Peshlakai, she was feeling anything but cheerful. Her mother had been difficult, full of those personal questions that are tough to answer. Was she absolutely sure about Jim Chee? Hadn't she heard that his Slow Talking Dinee clan produced unreliable husbands? Did Chee still intend to become a medicine man, a singer? Shouldn't she see about finding another job before getting married? Why was it Chee was still just a sergeant? And so forth. Finally, where were they going to live? Didn't Bernie respect the traditions of the Dineh? Chee would—at least he should—be joining their family; Bernie wouldn't be joining his. He should be coming to live with Bernie. Had she found them a place? So it went—a very stressful visit that dragged on until she agreed to drive down and have a talk with Hosteen Peshlakai, who as her mother's elder brother was Bernie's clan father. It was a promise Bernie had been happy to make, and not just to break off the maternal interrogation. She admired Peshlakai, loved him, too. A wonderful man.

Wonderful late-summer morning, too, with a great white many-turreted castle of cumulus cloud building over the Carrizo Mountains and another potential rainstorm brewing over the Chuskas. Usually such dramatic beauty and the promise of blessed rain would have had Bernie happily humming one of her many memorized tunes. Today they merely reminded her of the drought-stricken look of the slopes where Towering House clan sheep herds grazed, and that the summer monsoon rains were too late to do much good, and that even these promising-looking clouds would probably drift in the wrong direction.

She could blame this unusually negative mood on all those probing maternal inquiries, but it was the "missed call" message on her cell phone when she returned to the truck that made her start thinking hard, and painfully, about her mother's questions.

The caller was Jim Chee. The tone was strictly official—Sergeant Chee speaking with no hint of sentimental affection.

"Bernie, I won't be getting to your place today." Then came a terse explanation about having to help Cowboy Dashee help Dashee's cousin, which required going down into the Hopi Salt Shrine area in the Grand Canyon, where he "might have to spend a day or two."

At least, Bernie was thinking, he didn't address me as Officer Manuelito. But there certainly was some wisdom in some of her mother's questions. Would she, as her mother had wondered, be continuing her role as underling to a master by marrying her sergeant? Maybe mothers did know best. Bernie didn't think so. Probably not. She wished that telephone call had included at least some hint of regret. Or of intimacy. And why didn't he at least suggest she might want to come along?

Perhaps Chee didn't remember her chattering away one day about how exciting it was when the science teacher took her sixth-grade class on a field trip into the Canyon. Taught them about its geology and biology, the different kind of frogs, etc., how the heat reflected off south-facing cliffs made different species of plants grow, etc., how thrilling it had been. Forgetting that conversation would be some sort of an excuse for him not inviting her to go along. But that would mean he didn't pay attention when she talked. That was just as bad. Maybe worse.

At Shiprock, Bernie turned south onto old Highway 666, decided Peshlakai could wait. She would waste a minute, drive up the road along the San Juan and see if Chee's car was parked by his mobile home by the riverbank. It probably wouldn't be on this working day, but if he wasn't home it would give her a chance to take a private look at his place.

She parked where Chee's car would have been, got out, leaned against the door, and studied the place. The trailer looked as dented, grimy, and decrepit as she remembered. But the windows were clean, she noticed, and she credited Jim with that since he was the only occupant. The axles, where the wheels would be replaced when time came to move, were covered with canvas to protect them from rain, rust, or whatever would damage such machinery. The little "pet flap" Chee had installed on the bottom of the entry door was still there even though the cat was long since gone.

The flap revived a memory of how Chee's mind worked. The cat, pregnant and abandoned by a tourist, had been chased up one of the trees shading his trailer. Chee had rescued it. While refusing to adopt it as a pet (which would violate nature's sacred relationship between human and feline), he had arranged a feeding and watering place near his door, giving her some chance to survive until she learned rural ways while respecting her right to be a free and independent cat—and not a slave to his human species. After Cat, as Chee named it, barely escaped another coyote attack, he cut the hole in his door, attached the flap, and kept it open with the feeding dish just inside until Cat established her habit of coming in to eat, drink, or elude coyotes. But the arrangement remained strictly formal.

About ten feet down aluminum-siding from the door, a metal patch had been taped to the wall, covering a hole. A deranged woman, thinking Chee was a Skinwalker and had witched her, had blasted the hole (just over the cot where Chee slept) with her shotgun. Cat, ears attuned to stalking coyotes, heard the intruder coming and dived under the flap, awakening Chee and— as Chee told the story—saving his life.

Remembering Chee telling his version of Cat's heroism caused Bernadette Manuelito to produce her first smile of the day. She walked around the trailer, trotted up the four steps to the plank patio he'd attached to the river side of it, sat in his deck chair, and considered the view.

The sound of the San Juan, flowing almost directly below, would be tamed to just a murmur by autumn. It had been a light-snow winter in the Southern Rockies. Thus the contribution being made by the Animas River upstream was minimal this season. The San Juan itself was still providing its final flow into the diversion channels of the Navajo Irrigation Project. The San Juan here—alas, all of this portion of the great

Colorado Plateau—was thirstily awaiting the storms of winter. Or, even better, arrival of the rains of the summer's already-tardy monsoon season.

Well, maybe they were coming now. Last night's TV weather forecast had suggested that the great bubble of high pressure over the high desert was finally breaking up. Bernie found herself relaxing, her normal optimism restoring itself, discounting her mother's concerns about whether Jim Chee would be incurably a sergeant, remembering his smile, his tendency to break the white-man rules in favor of Navajo kindness, remembering his arm around her, his kiss. Ah, well, Bernie thought, she would continue her drive down to Coyote Canyon and up the canyon to Hosteen Peshlakai's hogan. She was pretty sure that Peshlakai would tell her what she was hoping to hear—his wise Navajo version of "love conquers all."

And the clouds were building up in the west. That was always a reason for optimism.

7

Joanna Craig was determined not to let her impatience show. This was far too important. This was the only really important thing in her life. Ever. She couldn't risk alienating this tough-looking little Indian sitting there by the window, examining the back of his hand to keep from looking at her. She had to suppress her impatience. And the anger she had been suppressing for much of her life. She had always managed that before. She would manage it now.

And somehow the irony of all of it seemed to make where this was leading foredoomed and inevitable. Even this room. The way it was decorated for another generation. As if designed to take her back to the day when her father was killed, to make her remember that. Not that she didn't always remember it, what she had read about it in that thick bundle of newspaper clippings she had found in the closet after her mother's death. The sad stories, the dramatic news photos of the wreckage of the two planes made it seem that she had actually seen it. Now the scenes her imagination had created had a reality of their own. Her father in his first-class seat, eager to be reunited with her mother, loving her, thinking of the honeymoon they would take, looking down into the vast colorscape of the canyon's cliffs, and then seeing that other airliner emerging from a cloud, imagining him knowing a terrible death was just a second away. Then Joanna had always fled from that thought to the way life might have been. Should have been.

Billy Tuve was still studying the back of his hand, ignoring what she had just said to him about the wealth those diamonds could bring to him. Wealth seemed to be something that didn't interest him. He wanted to talk about his mother being worried, about how good it was that this cousin of his, this deputy sheriff, was trying to help him.

"Mr. Tuve," Joanna said. "I guess I didn't really explain why I came out here to put up the money to get you out of jail. I just made it sound like I was doing it because I knew you didn't kill that man for his diamond. Just because I wanted to see you treated justly. I can see why you wouldn't believe that, and I don't think you did."

Billy Tuve looked up, produced a faint smile.

"No," he said. "I have known quite a few white people. There's always something they're after."

"So you know I have my own reason. I want to tell you what that is and ask you if you can help me."

Tuve stared at her, nodded.

Now he was interested. At least curious.

"That diamond you got from that man in the canyon, that diamond they accuse you of stealing from the storekeeper, that diamond used to belong to my father. His name was John Clarke. Mama called him Johnnie, and he was on one of those airplanes that ran together over the canyon all those years ago. Before either one of us was born. That was John's business. Diamonds. He was bringing a case full of them back to New York, and one of them was for my mother. They were getting married as soon as he got home. That diamond was going to be her present."

Tuve considered that. "Oh?"

"But he got killed," Joanna said. "She didn't get it."

Tuve just looked at her, thinking about that. Nodded, with that expression that said he understood.

"Well," Joanna said. "They'd got together when they got engaged. She was already pregnant."

Tuve shrugged.

"They had a big wedding planned. Dress fitted. Invitations sent out. Lots of—" She stopped, trying to imagine a Hopi wedding, knowing she didn't have a clue about that.

"Anyway, after my father died, his family wouldn't have anything to do with her. Wouldn't have anything to do with me, either." She stopped. Why would Tuve care about any of this? But he seemed to. Seemed eager to hear more. His face was slightly lopsided, as if his right cheekbone had been smashed or something. It made his expression a little hard to read, but now he looked sympathetic. He shook his head again.

"Not even your grandparents," Tuve said. "That's too bad."

"They lived a long ways off," she said, and suddenly she realized she really, really wanted to tell this homely little man everything. He was obviously mentally retarded. But he'd been hurt, too. He could understand that.

"Yes," Tuve was saying. "My grandmother taught me a lot of things. My grandfather taught me how to ride, how to hunt rabbits. When I was in the hospital, they both came. And they always brought me things."

And so Joanna kept talking. Talking about how, when she had reached puberty, her mother told her the whole story, of her love affair with John Clarke, about their wedding plans, about going to the Clarke family's huge house after John's death and knowing right away that she wasn't welcome. About how coldly they had treated her—especially John's father. How she had left with nobody saying good-bye.

"Nobody even told her good-bye?" Tuve asked. That seemed to touch a memory.

Joanna had ordered lunch from room service. She talked on and on while they waited for it, about becoming a nurse, the death of the elderly engineering professor she had married, and about how after she had buried him, she'd come to the Grand Canyon to see if she could find the grave of her own father.

"I went to the cemetery they established at

Northern Arizona University, but that was for all those killed in one of the airplanes—a great granite headstone with all the names on it was there, but my father was on the other plane and his name wasn't there. So I came to the Grand Canyon, to the National Park Service Center. They have the names of those on his plane there at the Shrine of the Ages monument, where they buried body parts they couldn't identify. An old man there told me that the plane my father was on had flown right into the wall of the cliff and sort of splattered, and then burned, but some of the bodies were thrown out, all torn up. I told him that my father told my mother he was bringing home a whole container full of diamonds for his company in New York, and the best one of them would be for her ring, and that he had the case all those diamonds were in handcuffed to his arm so nobody could steal it."

With that, Joanna paused, wiped away a tear with the back of her hand. It was the ideal place for weeping to impress Tuve, but she hadn't consciously planned it. The tears had been spontaneous. Since her childhood she had loved this man whom she was doomed never to see. And cried for him. Or perhaps it was for what his death had cost her.

"Sorry," she said. "Anyway, the man told me that a lot of the bodies were all torn up, or burned up, and just put in mass graves. And he said people used to talk about one of the Grand Canyon people seeing an arm caught in a brush pile below one of the rapids that had a case of some sort handcuffed to it, but before it could be retrieved, it washed away." She paused again, studying Tuve. His expression was blank.

"Do you see what I'm getting at?"

Tuve was silent a moment. Then: "No."

"The man who you got the diamond from must have found that arm, and that case locked to it."

"Yeah," Tuve said, smiling. "You want me to help you find that man so you can find the diamonds. The ones that would make you rich."

"I want to find the man so I can find the arm," Joanna said. "I want to give it back to my father. Bury it where he is buried at the Shrine of the Ages. But if we find the arm, we will also find the diamonds, and that will prove you told the truth to the police and you didn't steal it."

That provoked another thoughtful silence. "Yes," he said. "But about what you told me about burying that arm bone. Do you think that would make a difference?"

"I have dreams about it," Joanna said. "I don't see my father in them. I have never seen him. But I hear him. And he is crying for that arm. So it will quit hurting. So the pain will go away. So he can sleep in peace."

Tuve considered. "You dream that a lot?"

"All the time," Joanna said.

"Yes," Tuve said. "Sometimes I am afraid to go to sleep. The dreams scare me."

"I know. I woke up once just cold and shaking. In the dream I had been sleeping under a bridge, and I couldn't find my purse, and I didn't know anyplace to go where I could wash, or get warm." She looked up at Tuve.

He seemed fascinated.

"And the rats were all around me," she said.

"Sometimes it's terrible," Tuve said. "Once I dreamed I was under the horse and I couldn't get out, and my head, well, it was almost flat, like a plate. And my eyeballs were out and there was no place I could put them."

Joanna shuddered at that. "That's worse than

any I can remember. I think you understand why I think you and I should help each other."

Someone was tapping on the door. Room service, Joanna thought. She glanced at Tuve. "Should I let them in?"

"It's all right," Tuve said. "I understand."

8

The thunderstorm that had been moving steadily toward Gallup from the southwest produced a dazzling flash of lightning just as Navajo County Deputy Sheriff Cowboy Dashee and Sergeant Jim Chee of the Navajo Tribal Police climbed out of Chee's car in the parking lot. A sharp clap of thunder came two seconds later, the characteristic ozone scent generated by electrically charged air, and then a gust of dusty wind that made the jail door hard to open and blew Chee's hat into the room ahead of him.

"Well, now," said the woman behind the desk. "Look what the wind blew in. I was hoping we'd finally get some rain."

Dashee said, "It's coming. Today's the day the Zunis are having their rodeo. They did their rain dance last night."

Chee rescued his cap, said, "Hello, Mrs. Sosi."

Mrs. Sosi was laughing. "I asked one of them about that last year when they got rained out again. Told him they should do the dance after the rodeo. He said the rain-outs kept the cowboys from getting hurt. Cut down the medical bills. Did you two come in to get out of the weather?"

"I want to talk to one of your tenants," Dashee said. "Billy Tuve. He's my cousin."

"Tuve?" Sosi said, frowning. She checked the roster on the desk in front of her. "Mr. Tuve is a popular man today. But you're too late. He bonded out about an hour ago."

"He what?! Wasn't that bond set at fifty thousand dollars? Was it lowered? Tuve couldn't have come up with any property valuable enough to cover that. And I guarantee he didn't have the five thousand he'd have needed to cover the bond company fee."

Mrs. Sosi looked down at her records, then looked up with an expression that registered amazed disbelief. "And it was a cash bond," she said.

"Cash? Fifty thousand in cash?"

"Same as cash. Registered, certified cashier's check," Mrs. Sosi said. "Bank of America."

Dashee's reaction to all this was shock.

"Who did it?" Chee asked.

"A woman. Just about middle-aged. Nice looking. I never saw her before." She glanced at the record book. "Ms. Joanna Craig. That mean anything to you?"

"Not to me," Dashee said.

"She wasn't local? Where was she from?"

"Well, she used a New York City bank account. She said she was representing Mr. Tuve, and I think maybe there was a lawyer with her."

Dashee was looking baffled.

"Did Tuve know her?" Chee asked.

"He seemed as surprised as you do," Mrs. Sosi said. "But he walked right out with her. Climbed into the car she was driving."

"What kind of car?" Chee asked. "Going where?"

"She said she was staying at the El Rancho Hotel. The car? It looked like one of those Ford sedans Avis rents out at the airport."

"I can't believe this," Dashee said. "I think we better go find him."

Chee held up his hand. "This lawyer with her. Was he in the car, too?"

"Just her and Tuve. And this other fella, I don't know he was a lawyer. He just came in earlier. Big blond guy and he said he came from Tuve's family, but he sure wasn't no Hopi. Just said he wanted to talk to Tuve about getting money put up for his bond. The deputy took him back there awhile, and pretty soon he came out and said thank you, and went on out. That's the last I saw of him."

"But he was with the woman?"

She shook her head and laughed. "We don't get an awful lot of out-of-town traffic in here, so I just connected them. Both interested in getting Tuve out. But I don't know," Mrs. Sosi said. "Now I sort of doubt it. He was gone before she got here. I never saw them together."

"Let's go," Dashee said. "Come on. Let's go talk to Tuve. Find out what this is all about."

The ride up Railroad Avenue to the El Rancho was a splash through a rain mixed with occasional flurries of popcorn-size hail.

"What do you think, Jim?" Dashee said. "What sort of mess has the silly bastard got himself into? I can't think of a thing he could do that would make him worth that much money to anyone."

"You think maybe he actually did shoot that tourist shop operator?" But Chee answered his own question with a negative head shake. "No.

That wouldn't add up. Wouldn't make somebody in New York come out here to buy him out for that much money." He shook his head, thinking. "I was wondering who that man was. You have any ideas about that?"

"I don't. Billy didn't shoot anybody," Dashee said. "Billy was a good kid. Not the brightest bulb in the house after he got his head hurt. But he never quit being nice. He used to ride in that rodeo for kids. Did calf roping. Then his horse fell on him when he was twelve or so. Rolled over his head. Skull fracture. Longtime coma. The whole thing. And when he finally got out of the hospital, he wasn't quite right anymore. To tell the truth, he was sort of retarded even before that. But he was always a good boy."

"Didn't change his personality?"

"Seemed like it made him even better. He did things for everybody. Kept firewood cut for his neighbors. Didn't make trouble even when he was drinking. And I think he might have quit that drinking."

"Remember what we got together to talk to him about?" Chee said. "About that expensive jewel. I think all this must have something to do with that damned diamond."

"Probably," Dashee said, and produced a dour chuckle. "And Tuve told me that thing was a phony. He said he knew everybody thought he was dumb, but he wasn't stupid enough to think that was a real diamond."

The El Rancho Hotel had been built in the long-gone golden days of Hollywood movie studios. One of the big names in the industry had financed it to house the stars and production crews making the cowboy-and-Indian films that filled the theaters in the 1930s and '40s. Despite some refurbishing, it showed its heritage. Its walls were still lined with autographed publicity photographs of the Hoot Gibson/Roy Rogers generations, and its atmosphere was rich with old and dusty glamour.

"Yes," the desk clerk told Dashee. "A Ms. Joanna Craig. She has 201. We call that the Clark Gable Suite. You want me to ring her for you?"

"Please," Dashee said.

"No, wait," Chee said. "You know how Joanna loves surprises. What's the suite number again? We'll just go up and knock."

Dashee was looking puzzled as they went up the stairs.

"What was that all about?"

"I'm just being cynical," Chee said. "Thought we'd surprise her. Who is this woman, anyway?"

Suite 201 was on the second floor, on the corridor overlooking the hotel lobby. Through the door came the faint sound of conversation. Chee knocked. Waited. The door opened. A small blond woman in a trim dark blue suit stood looking at him, then past him at Dashee, expression stern.

"I thought you were room service," she said. "Who are you?"

Chee was reaching for his identification. "And I presume you are Ms. Joanna Craig," he said.

"You're a policeman," she said.

"I am Sergeant Jim Chee," Chee said, and showed her his identification folder.

"And I'm a cousin of Mr. Tuve," Cowboy said. He waved at the young man sitting slumped in an overstuffed chair by the window and said, "Good to see you, Billy. How you doing?"

The man returned the gesture, with a happy grin of recognition.

"I would ask you in," Joanna Craig said, "but Mr. Tuve and I are engaged in a conversation. It's business."

"We have business, too," Chee said. "Police business."

"I don't understand this," she said, looking sterner than ever. "I am legally representing Mr. Tuve. And he is free on bond. Free as a bird until he is called in to testify, or this ridiculous charge is dropped."

"I'm not here on police business," Dashee said. "I'm doing family business. Billy Tuve's mother and my mother are sisters. We're kinfolks. Cousins. I need to talk to my cousin Billy."

"Hey, Cowboy," Tuve said. "You're looking good. Did Mama send you?"

Ms. Craig considered this. Looked at Chee. "It could be that we have a shared interest? I want to clear Mr. Tuve of this homicide-robbery charge. You, too?"

"Yes, exactly," Chee said.

Craig was looking past him now at the arriving room service cart. She stood aside, motioned it in, and extended the same gesture to Chee and Dashee.

"Would you care to join us? Have some coffee, or tea, or whatever. We'll just tell the man to bring it up."

"No, thanks," Chee said. "We'd just like to ask Mr. Tuve for some information."

"Make yourselves at home," she said. "Mr. Tuve and I will have our lunch, but go ahead with your questions."

Chee and Dashee looked at each other. Dashee shrugged.

"The trouble is what we want to discuss with Mr. Tuve is police business. It's confidential."

Craig smiled. "Confidential. Of course. No one will hear it except the four of us. You two, Mr. Tuve, and"—she tapped herself on her shirt-front—"myself. His legal representative."

Chee looked skeptical, glanced at Tuve. Tuve, he thought, had the look of an athlete—short like many Hopis, hard muscles, built like a wrestler.

"Mr. Tuve. Did you retain Ms. Craig as your attorney?"

Tuve looked puzzled. "I don't think so. I don't have any money."

"My work is related to the interests of a tax-exempt public charity foundation," Craig said, her face slightly flushed. "My interest is in protecting Mr. Tuve from unjust prosecution." She turned toward Tuve. "Mr. Tuve, do you wish to talk to these gentlemen?"

Tuve shrugged. "Sure. Why not? Looking good, Cowboy. How'd you hear about this trouble? I'll bet my mother sent you over here to get me."

Chee sighed, defeated. "Okay," he said. "Ms. Craig, this is Deputy Dashee, with the Navajo County Sheriff's Department." Craig, he guessed, would not know Navajo County was across the border in Arizona, devoid of any jurisdiction here. "I presume you know that the only material evidence the state has to connect Mr. Tuve with the robbery-homicide at Zuni is a diamond he attempted to pawn. We are hoping to find concrete evidence that Mr. Tuve got that diamond exactly as he claims. To check it out, we want to get some more details from him about the circumstances."

Craig considered this. Nodded. "Have a seat," she said. "Or join us at the table." She moved her purse off a chair and put it on a closet shelf. The purse was a large and fashionable leather affair and it seemed to Chee remarkably heavy, even for its size.

The Clark Gable Suite offered numerous comfortable choices for seating—a richly covered sofa, three overstuffed chairs, an ottoman, and four standard dining room chairs around the table. The windows offered a view to the east and north of the mainline railroad tracks, now carrying a seemingly endless line of freight cars toward California, the traffic flowing by on Interstate Highway 40, and beyond all that the spectacular red cliffs that had attracted Hollywood here to produce its horse operas so common through the middle years of the century. Through a double doorway Chee could see into the suite's handsome bedroom.

He selected an overstuffed chair and seated himself. Dashee, wearing a "what the hell" expression, chose the sofa.

"We're going to ask Mr. Tuve some questions, then," Chee said. "And it appears we have a mutual interest in the answers. But first we'd like to know why the organization you represent has a fifty-thousand-dollar interest in this."

Joanna Craig pondered this a moment, studying Chee. "What organization is that?" she asked.

"The one you just mentioned that sent you here to protect Mr. Tuve. The one that gave you the check to pay for bonding Mr. Tuve out of jail."

"Its identity is confidential."

"The check you provided to pay for the bond was written on a Bank of America account. It had your name on it."

Joanna Craig sighed, shrugged, nodded.

"Why did your employers send you here?" Chee asked. "Why do they have a fifty-thousand-dollar interest in Mr. Tuve?"

"You'll have to ask them." She smiled at him.

"I will," Chee said. "Give me the name and address."

She considered that awhile, shook her head.

"I would, but they'd just tell you it's none of your business. Just waste your time."

For a while the room was silent. Through the windows came the diminishing sound of thunder, already dim and distant, the jumbled noise of truck traffic on Interstate 40, and the nearer sound of cars on Railroad Avenue. Inside the room only Cowboy Dashee chuckling, and the click of his spoon as Tuve stirred sugar into his cup of coffee.

"Well, then," Chee said. "I guess we might as well just get down to business. Mr. Tuve, would you please tell us how you got that diamond."

"Like I already told the sheriff and that FBI man, an old man gave it to me," Tuve said. "Didn't look like a Hopi. Old. Had a lot of long white hair. Looked Indian, though, but maybe not. Maybe a Havasupai. They live down there in the bottom of the canyon, across the river, but they ought not be around our Salt Shrine. That's just for Bear Clan people."

Billy Tuve took a sip of his coffee, glowering over the rim of the cup at the thought of that.

"Let's skip back, then," Chee said. "Start from what you were doing down in the canyon, where you said it happened, and take it from there."

"Some of it I can't talk about. It's kiva business. Secret."

"Then when you come to the secret part, just tell it to Dashee. In Hopi. That will keep it confidential."

"We're both in the Bear Clan but we didn't get initiated into the same kiva," Tuve said. "There's some of it I couldn't tell him, either."

"Well, just do what your conscience lets you do, then."

Joanna Craig frowned.

Tuve nodded and began his account, Hopi fashion, from the beginning.

Chee slumped back into his chair, relaxing, getting comfortable, preparing for a long, long session. He'd listen carefully when Tuve got through the religious preamble and began to discuss receipt of the diamond. Until then he'd consider whether Craig was actually a lawyer.

Anyone could have posted Tuve's bond. He'd ponder what she was doing here. If the opportunity arose, he'd try to find out what caused her purse to seem so heavy, even for its size. A tape recorder? A pistol? Meanwhile, he'd enjoy himself. He concentrated on thinking about Bernadette Manuelito. Happy, happy thoughts. About fixing up his place on the San Juan with her. They'd have to move in a double bed. Couldn't use those little narrow foldout bunks after you're a married couple. Have to get some curtains on the windows. Things like that.

Tuve was talking now of having to go to a meeting in the kiva of the Hopi religious society to which he belonged. He was being considered for membership in an ancient organization that non-Hopis called the Bow Society, which wasn't its real name. Anyway, he was going to take part in an initiation. That involved a pilgrimage by potential members from their village on Second Mesa all the way to the south rim of the Grand Canyon. From there they made the perilous climb down the cliffs—a descent of more than four thousand feet—to the bottom near where the Little Colorado pours into the Colorado River. But first Billy Tuve had to deal with the ceremonial eagle, tell Miss Craig how it had been collected from one of the nests guarded by his society, how a shaman brought it in, prayers were said, the proper herbs were smoked. Then the eagle was smothered, plucked, sprinkled with blessed cornmeal, and, as Tuve expressed it, "sent home to join his own spirits with our prayers to help him lead us on a safe journey."

Chee let his attention drift and his gaze shift from Ms. Craig's face to the window behind her. The rainstorm had drifted east, and the red cliffs that formed their walls north of Gallup were streaked now with sunlight and shadow, varying from dark crimson where the rain had soaked them to pale pink where it hadn't, leaving a dozen shades in between. And above them another great tower of white was climbing, with the west wind blowing mist from it, forming an anvil shape at its top and producing a thin screen of ice crystals against the dark blue sky. Some other parts of the Navajo Nation would be getting rain.

Chee was remembering a chant a Zuni girlfriend had taught him from a prayer of her tribe's A'shiwannis religious order:

**Send out your cloud towers to live
with us,**

**stretch out your watery hands of mist.
Let us embrace one another.**

This had been before Chee met Bernadette
Manuelito, and fallen in love with her, so that
now even rain clouds caused him to think of her.
Thinking now of embracing Bernie, instead of
listening to Tuve, who was still talking, but not
talking about diamonds. Who needed diamonds
with ice crystals glittering against the blue, blue
sky. With Bernie willing to marry him. With the
time for that already established.

Behind him Tuve was now droning through
the required ceremonialism of the Salt Trail,
talking about feathers and prayer sticks being
properly painted to be used as required at the
springs, shrines, and sacred places they would be
passing. And for Billy Tuve, conditioned as he
was to getting the details of Hopi ceremonialism
precisely correct, this took patient listening. And
more time was taken because he often nodded
apologetically to Chee and Ms. Craig, and
shifted into Hopi to speak directly to Dashee,
thus preserving the secrets of the tribe's religions. When special affairs of his own kiva became involved, Tuve simply showed Dashee the
palms of his hands and went silent.

Getting this ceremonial procession from Tuve's village on Second Mesa to the canyon rim and then to the riverbank involved describing several more stops for prayers and offerings, the placing of painted feathers in the proper places with the proper songs, and putting prayer sticks where the proper spirits traditionally visited. By the time Tuve had brought them to the Hopi shrines at the tribe's cliff-bottom salt deposits, Joanna Craig had looked at her watch three times that Chee had noticed. Navajo fashion, he hadn't glanced at his own. Tuve would finish when he finished.

And, at last, Tuve finished. He spent less than a minute on the ceremony itself, declared that the group had collected the necessary salt at the Salt Shrine and clays of various colors along the cliff walls needed for various undescribed purposes.

"Then I met the man who gave me the diamond," he said. He leaned back in his chair and looked at each of them. Now it was their turn to talk.

Dashee looked at Chee, waited.

Chee frowned, considering.

Miss Craig said, "You told me you didn't know this man. Is that right?"

Tuve nodded. "He didn't say his name."

"Describe him."

Tuve made an uncertain face. "Long time ago," he said. "Grandfather probably. Maybe even a great-grandfather. Old, I mean. Lots of white hair. Skinny. Sort of bent over. About as tall as Sergeant Chee there. Not a Hopi, I think. Some other kind of Indian. He had on worn-out blue jeans and a blue shirt and a raggedy jacket, and a gray felt hat. And he had a big wide leather belt with silver-looking conchas on it."

"How did you happen to meet him?"

Tuve scratched his ear, looked thoughtful. "I was digging out some of that blue clay. Chopping it out with a little thing I got to chop roots with." He looked at Craig, wondering if she'd understand. "Like that little shovel they use in the army. Short handle." He illustrated with his hands. "And the shovel part then can fold down." Another illustration, of folding and chopping. "Got it at one of those military surplus stores, and sharpened it up. Works good. Really cuts roots."

Tuve looked at Craig, awaiting approval. Didn't get it. Craig was looking at her watch again.

"And he walked up, or what?"

"He said something, and I looked over and he was standing there watching me dig clay. So I said something friendly. And he came up and wanted to see my digging tool. And I handed it to him and in a minute he said he would trade something to me for it. I said what, and he got a folding knife out of his pocket and showed me that. I said no. He said for me to wait and then he came back with that diamond in a little pouch. And we traded."

That said, Tuve nodded, looked down at his folded hands. End of story.

"All this talking with this old man," Craig said. "That was in English, or Hopi, or what?"

Tuve laughed. "I couldn't understand his words. So it went like this." He demonstrated with his hand and facial expressions.

"And where did he go after you swapped your shovel for his diamond?" Chee asked.

Tuve shrugged. "Down the canyon a little way, and then around the corner." He shrugged again.

Craig sighed, shook her head.

Chee cleared his throat, looked at Craig, saw no sign she had another question to ask.

"Do you remember where this happened?"

he asked. "I mean, exactly where you were digging the clay?"

"Sure," Tuve said. "It's real close to the place we leave prayer sticks and do our prayers for the Salt Mother. Down the river a little ways. Where we always dig that yellow clay for painting."

"Can you remember how long he was gone before he came back with the diamond?"

Tuve pondered. "It was just a little while."

"Can you tell us like how many minutes?"

Tuve looked baffled by that.

"Maybe long enough to smoke a cigarette?" Chee suggested. "Or a lot longer than that?"

"Didn't have any cigarettes," Tuve said.

"Okay, then," Chee said. "What did you get done while you waited? How much clay did you dig, for example."

"Didn't dig. I got out my water bottle, and I sat down on a sort of rocky shelf there and took a drink, and got my boot off and shook out the sand that got into it and put the boot back on, and then I sort of asked myself why I was sitting there waiting for this old fella when I didn't really want to trade my digging tool anyway, and got up to go and then he was back."

"Less than an hour?"

"Lot less than an hour. Maybe fifteen minutes."

"From what I know about you Hopis," Chee said, "you have your own special ceremonial trail down to those salt deposits. Is that the one you climbed down on that day?"

Tuve said something in Hopi to Dashee. Dashee nodded, said, "Yes. That's the one I was telling you about."

Craig was listening to all this, looking thoughtful.

"Mr. Tuve," she said. "I want you to take me down there. We have to find that man."

"Can't do that," Tuve said. He laughed. "Not unless you can get into the women's kiva. Have to be initiated, and that's after you know all the rules."

"What are they?"

"Women rules. They don't tell men."

"Well, can you tell me a way to get down there? It's the way to keep you out of jail," she said. "To find the man who gave you the diamond. We need to get him so he can testify he gave you that."

Tuve was shaking his head. "Can't do that," he said, still smiling. "Against the rules of the kiva."

"Can't you just explain it to the bishop, or whatever you call him? He'd understand."

Tuve's smile had faded away. He looked extremely serious, thinking. "No," he said. "Not unless it would be for something the spirits would like."

Craig stared at him. Checked Chee for comment. Got none. Glanced at Dashee. There was the mutter of thunder, very distant now. Their rainstorm was still drifting eastward.

"Something the spirits would like," Craig said. "Like helping somebody who has been hurt very bad. Somebody who really needs help. Would they like that?"

Tuve stared at her, looked at Dashee, a question on his face.

Dashee said, "We don't do it. Don't take white people down that trail. They are not initiated. They don't know the prayers to say, don't know what Masaw told us to do. If they go down for the wrong reason, with the wrong spirit, a Two Heart will make them fall."

Craig looked surprised, then interested. "Masaw? Who's that?"

Tuve ignored the question.

Dashee looked at Chee.

Chee shrugged. "I'm not a Hopi, you know,

but we Navajos understand that Masaw is their Guardian Spirit of the Underworld. Sometimes he's called Skeleton Man or Death Man because he taught the Hopis not to be afraid to die. Anyway, after the Hopis came up to the Earth Surface World, they say God made him sort of their guardian if I've got it right. And the Two Hearts are the sort of people who didn't quite make the transition from what they were in the underworld into the human form. Didn't get rid of the evil. Still have an extra animal heart. Sort of like the witches you white people talk about."

"Or like the witches Navajos call Skinwalkers," Dashee said, with a sardonic glance at Chee.

"Actually, we call them Long Lookers," Chee said, looking slightly apologetic. "And we have several versions of them."

"I think the rain's finished here for now," Dashee said, trying to change the subject. "Moving over to the Checkerboard Reservation."

"One more question," Chee said. "Mr. Tuve, who was that man who came to see you this morning?"

"I don't know him. He said his name was Jim Belshaw, and he said he wanted to know about getting me out of jail. And he wanted to talk to me about the diamond. He said he would come back later to get me out."

Tuve nodded toward Craig, who was watching this exchange. "I thought maybe this lady here sent him. She could tell you about him."

"I didn't send him," Craig said, looking startled and flustered. She glanced at Chee, a questioning look.

"Oh," Tuve said. "That seems funny."

She looked at Chee. "One of your people?"

"Not us," Chee said. "I don't know who he was. Neither did the court clerk."

"Well, anyway, then," Craig said to Tuve. "If you can't take me down the Salt Trail—and I really don't want to bother your Two Hearts—then we'll just get down there another way."

Chee noticed that she was smiling at Tuve as she said it.

9

The thunderstorm was gone from Gallup now, drifting away to bestow its blessing wherever the wind or Pueblo rain dances took it. One of Billy Tuve's numerous uncles had arrived to give him a ride back to Shungopovi on Second Mesa. Chee watched Joanna Craig chatting with Tuve, a conversation he didn't manage to overhear, and then giving him his instructions on the requirements of those free on bond. Chee gave Craig his police card and a request that she stay in touch. Then Dashee led the way out into the hotel parking lot to Chee's car.

"Look at it," Dashee said. "Clean. Didn't recognize it. I never saw it like that before. You can even make out that Navajo Nation symbol on the door."

"Get in, Cowboy," Chee said. "Let's get something to eat."

"And decide what to do," Dashee said. "What'd you think of that Craig woman?"

"How about you?" Chee said. "I noticed you were being uncharacteristically polite. I mean, hopping up and rushing over to get her purse and hand it to her."

"It was heavy," Dashee said.

"Yeah," Chee said. "I thought it would be. The way it looked."

"Maybe she's carrying a super makeup outfit, or a really old-fashioned cell telephone, or"—Dashee gave Chee a sidewise look—"maybe a pistol?"

"The pistol occurred to me," Chee said. "She's from the East, you know. A lot of Easterners worry about you Indians."

"Hey!" Dashee said. "We Hopis are the peaceful ones. You Navajos were the hostiles. And you were showing it again today."

"What do you mean by that?"

"You wouldn't let us eat lunch with Ms. Craig there at the hotel. So we just sat there in the chair and watched them eat."

"Good point," Chee said. "That wasn't very

smart." He turned his clean, rain-washed car into the Bob's Diner parking lot.

While they dined they agreed on several other points.

For one, Tuve would win no prizes for intellectual brilliance. His story about swapping his shovel for the diamond was not going to sound likely to a jury.

They weren't convinced themselves.

However, the prosecution seemed to have little genuine evidence against Tuve. The fingerprints he'd left in the store proved only that he'd been there on the fatal day, and the witnesses could prove little more than the same thing.

Their chances of finding Tuve's diamond donor, if he had ever existed, were minuscule.

"I guess we're agreed, then," Dashee said. "We'll hope Ms. Craig finds herself a good canyon-bottom guide and turns up the diamond donor. And we'll keep our eyes open for some sensible way to help Cousin Billy. And unless the FBI comes up with some sort of material evidence, we sort of doubt he'll need help, anyway."

"I'm not so sure about that," Chee said. "I'll bet they have something substantial."

Dashee grinned. "When in doubt, get some Hopis on the jury. We're a kind-hearted tribe."

"Generous, too," Chee said, handing Dashee the lunch check and pushing back from the table. "I've got to get back to Shiprock now. Bernie wants me to go look at a couple of places she thinks might be right for us to live in."

"What's wrong with your trailer?" Dashee asked, trying to suppress a grin. "It's really handy for you there. Right next to the Shiprock garbage dump, for example."

"And right next to the San Juan River flowing by," Chee said. "I think it's a pretty place. I'm going to talk her into it. But first I've got to look at what she's looking at."

But when Chee parked under the cottonwood shading his front door from the setting sun, the old trailer looked shabby and disreputable, putting a dent in his cheerful mood.

The mood improved when he saw the light blinking on his answering machine. It would be Bernie. Just hearing her voice brightened the day. Alas, it wasn't Bernie. It was the familiar voice of Joe Leaphorn, the legendary lieutenant, formally identifying himself as if he hadn't known Chee about forever.

"I hear from some sheriff's office people that you're trying to help Cowboy Dashee's cousin. If that's true, you might want to call me. It turns

out that Shorty McGinnis—You remember him.
Grouchy old fellow. Ran Short Mountain Trading Post. Well, he has a diamond story a lot like
the one your Billy Tuve tells. It might be helpful,
if you're interested."

As usual, Leaphorn was right. Chee was interested. He glowered at the telephone, dealing
with memories of other interesting calls from the
legendary lieutenant. Most of them had come
while he was working as Leaphorn's gofer in his
Criminal Investigation Office. They had tended
to lead to trouble and always meant a lot of hard
work. Some of it, admittedly, proved interesting
and fruitful, but this was not the time for that.
This was time to be with Bernie.

Chee walked away from the telephone, out
into the shady side of the trailer to a favorite
place of his—the remains of a fallen cottonwood
tree the trunk of which had long since lost its
bark and had been worn smooth by years of being sat upon. Chee sat upon it again and looked
down at the San Juan flowing below. A coyote
was out early, stalking something on the river's
opposite bank. He thought about Bernie and his
future with her. A pair of mallards feeding in the
shallows spotted the coyote and squawked into

flight. But the coyote wasn't hunting them. It continued its furtive way into a brushy growth of Russian olive. Stalking a rabbit, Chee guessed, or perhaps someone's pet dog or a feral cat. That thought reminded him of the cat that had moved in with him once, in another time, when he'd sat on this old log and considered whether he should accept what amounted to a counteroffer from Mary Landon. Yes, she had said, she would marry him. She had already planned on that. She'd already rejected the contract renewal she'd been offered at the Crownpoint Elementary School and was preparing to move back to Wisconsin. He could accept that job offer he'd had from the FBI and they would raise their children wherever they put him until they could arrange a transfer to the Milwaukee office. About his dream of becoming a shaman, a medicine person among the Navajos? Surely he'd already outgrown that idea, hadn't he?

The coyote was no longer visible to Chee. But there was a sudden flurry of activity in the brush and a dirty tabby cat scurried out of it and up an adjoining tree to safety. The coyote gave up the pursuit. Coyotes were too wise to engage in hopeless competitions.

And so are Navajos, Chee thought. Instead we endure, and we survive. But now Chee was thinking of another cat.

This one, skinny and ragged, had shown up around his trailer one autumn, attracted by food scraps he'd left out for squirrels. It wore a pretty collar—an animal raised as a pet, then abandoned with no survival skills and handicapped by pregnancy. He had put out food for the terrified beast and it quickly became a regular visitor. Then one of the neighborhood coyotes scented cat and began hunting it. Chee cut a cat-sized entry in his door and lured the animal through it with sardines. Soon the door flap became its emergency route to safety when a coyote prowled. Only when winter froze the San Juan and the snow began did it move in to spend the nights, still keeping a cautious distance from Chee. Thus they lived together, Chee serving as food provider, Cat operating as feline watchdog, bolting in with a clatter when a coyote (or any visitor) approached the trailer. Otherwise they ignored each other.

The relationship perfectly fit Chee Navajo traditionalism. Natural harmony required all species, be they human, hamster, hummingbird, snake, or scorpion, to respect each other's roles in the natural world. He saw no more justification in pretending to own a "pet" than he did in human slavery. Both violated the harmony of the system and thus were immoral. However, this cat presented a problem. It had been spoiled for a career as a naturally feral cat, not having been taught to hunt its food by its mother or how to evade other predators. Worse, it had been declawed—a cruel and barbarious custom. It could no longer adjust to the world into which it had been left. Chee understood that. That, too, was natural. He could not adjust to the world of Wisconsin dairy farming which Mary Landon planned for him. And Mary could not imagine raising her blond, blue-eyed children in his world. And so when her letters began arriving from Stevens Point, Wisconsin, beginning "Dear Jim" instead of "Darling," Chee put Cat in an airline-approved pet cage and sent it to her—out of the landscape of claw and fang, into a world in which animals were transformed from independent fellows into pets of their masters. With her Christmas card, Mary had sent him a picture of Cat on a sofa with her and her Wisconsin husband. Cat was now named Alice, and Mary was still so beautiful that he knew he would never quite forget her.

Chee rose from the log, went into his trailer, and retrieved the photograph from his desk drawer. He studied it, confirming his memory. Another moment of sorting produced a photograph of Janet Pete. Another sort of beauty. Not the soft, warm, sensual, farm-girl karma of Mary here. Janet was high-fashion, Ivy League law school chic. The word now was **cool**, in the sophisticated sense. She had been the court-appointed public defender of a murder suspect when he met her, an honor grad of a noted law school who had a yen for a seat someday on the Supreme Court. Her Navajo father had provided her the Pete name, her perfect complexion and classic bone structure. But her New England socialite mother had formed the Janet he knew, formed her in a world of high fashion, very important people, and a layered, sophisticated ruling class.

Janet smiled at him now out of the photograph, dark eyes, dark hair beautifully framing a perfect face, slender, an image of grace. Chee dropped both photographs back into the drawer and closed it, remembering how long it had taken him to understand Janet, to realize how smart she was, to realize how he fitted into her plans. Like Mary, she had (more or less) said yes.

He had obtained a videotape of a traditional Navajo wedding and took it to her apartment to explain it to her. Instead he learned the nuptials would be in a Washington cathedral with full pomp and ceremony. She had arranged to have the proper strings pulled to have herself transferred to a Justice Department job in Maryland. She had learned the U.S. Marshals Service had an opening there that exactly fit him. She was surprised that he was surprised.

The telephone rang.

Bernie, Chee thought. He picked it up. "Bernie," he said, "I've been—"

"It's Joe Leaphorn," the voice said. "I've been trying to reach you."

Chee exhaled. Said, "Oh, okay. I got your message. I was just going to call you. Tell me what McGinnis told you about the diamond."

"I will," Leaphorn said. "If you're still interested in that charge against Billy Tuve, I guess it's sort of good news. But now I've also got some bad news. I'll give you that first."

"Sure," Chee said.

"Sheriff Tomas Perez—you remember him, retired now. Anyway, I saw him down at the Navajo Inn at lunch. He told me he heard from his old undersheriff that they've got some more evidence against Tuve. Seems a former employee at that Zuni store reported that the manager there actually did have a big, valuable diamond in his stock. He said the boss had shown it to him several times. Was very proud of it."

"Oh," Chee said, thinking, Good-bye, Tuve.

Leaphorn awaited further comment. Got none.

"So it won't surprise you to hear that the victim's widow is claiming the diamond. The D.A. said she'd have to wait until after the trial and he'd need her to testify about it."

"Did she say she'd seen it, too?"

"Perez seemed to have that impression. But you know how it is. He's been out of the sheriff's job for three years now. Passing along third-hand stuff."

"Yeah," Chee said. "Do you know if Dashee knows about this?"

"Probably," Leaphorn said. "You know how that is, too. Bad news travels fast."

"Yep. It does."

"However, what Shorty told me makes it sound like Billy Tuve might actually have gotten that diamond down in the canyon. Shorty told me he got his own diamond—"

"Wait," Chee said. "Pardon the interruption. His own diamond? What does that mean?"

"Remember that Short Mountain burglary? Years ago? Shorty listed the diamond as part of the loss. He says he got it from a cowboy, a guy named Reno, who drifted through, gave it to him in exchange for some groceries and a ride into Page. This Reno told Shorty he'd traded one of those scabbard knives for it to an old man down in the Grand Canyon."

"About where in the canyon?"

"He said just down from the Little Colorado confluence."

"Well, now," Chee said. "That's interesting. That's the right general area."

"Must be very close to the place Tuve claims to have swapped off his folding shovel, right?"

"Right," Chee said. "I'll tell Dashee about this. Thanks."

"The even better news is you finally got wise enough to ask Bernadette to marry you. That correct?"

"It is."

Leaphorn chuckled. "They say third time's the charm. It is the third time, isn't it? First we heard you and that pretty blond girl teaching over at Crownpoint were getting married. And then we heard it was going to be the U.S. lawyer, Janet Pete. Both of those deals fell through. I hope you're not going to let Bernadette back out."

"Not if I can prevent it," Chee said.

"Well, I'm glad for you. Glad for both of you. She's a prize. It took you way too long to realize it."

"It wasn't that I didn't realize it. It was just— Just— Well, I don't know how to explain it."

"How about telling me it's none of my business. Or saying twice burned makes you triple careful. Anyway, congratulations. And tell Bernie everybody is happy for both of you."

"Well, thanks, Lieutenant. She's a great lady."

"You're going hunting, then? You think there's any hope of finding the diamond man? After all these years?"

"Not much, I guess. But what else can you do? Dashee and I talked about it, agreed it seemed hopeless, but if he's heard what you've just told me, I'm dead certain he's going to go hunting, and just as certain he'll want me to help—even though he probably won't ask me."

"I see your point," Leaphorn said. "Shorty

told me a couple of other things that might be helpful." He told Chee what Reno had said about meeting his diamond man at the mouth of a cave up one of those narrow little slots that drain runoff water down the cliffs into the Colorado River, about the diamond being in a snuff can, and the case from which the old man took it, containing several such cans.

"That's odd," Chee said.

"I thought so, too. But this old fellow had taken a smaller diamond out of a different snuff can. So maybe they're his storage units. And the can he gave Reno was in a leather pouch. Sort of like a medicine pouch."

"He was an Indian? What kind?"

"Shorty said Reno didn't know. But he didn't speak much English. And gave some hand signals saying the diamonds came out of an airplane crash."

"The pouch. Was that like one of ours?"

"About the same. But it had a sort of Anasazi-looking symbol stitched into it. Big figure with a tiny head, very broad upper torso, tiny stick legs."

"Any ideas about that?"

"I don't know. Maybe a clan totem, or a symbol of one of his tribe's spirits."

"Didn't look like any of the tribal figures you'd recognize, then?"

"No, but I've never had much contact with any of those tribes that far down the Colorado." Leaphorn chuckled. "I sort of neglected to give the pouch back to Shorty when I returned his diamond. Thought I'd show it to Louisa when she gets back. She's down in the canyon now, collecting her oral histories from the Havasupais."

"Well, thanks again," Chee said. "I guess I'll have to actually find that guy and ask him about it. And if something comes up and you need to find me, you have my cell phone number."

"Ah. Yeah. I think I wrote it down."

That concluded the conversation and left Chee to decide what to do about it. He'd call Dashee, of course. Discuss it with him. Find out what he wanted to do. But first he had to call Bernie.

He dialed her number. Thinking what he could have told Leaphorn if he wanted to confess the truth. He could have said he hadn't told Bernie he loved her a long time ago because he was afraid. Cowardice prevented it. It hurt when he learned that Mary Landon didn't want him. She wanted the dairy farmer she could make out of him. Lonely again after that. It hurt even more when he finally understood that he was just the token Navajo to Janet, someone to be taken back to Washington and civilized. Even lonelier than before. And when he found Bernie, right under his nose, he knew here was his chance. The really right one. He loved everything about her. But he was too damned scared to make the move. What if she rejected him? Mary and Janet, they'd found him someone they could mold into what they wanted. But he had found Bernie. And if she turned him down, he'd never find anyone like her. He'd never have a wife. He'd always be lonely, all the rest of his life.

He listened to Bernie's number ring nine times before he decided she wasn't home. And then he called Dashee. Told him the good news first, and then the bad news.

"I know," Dashee said. "I think that clerk and that widow are both lying, with the widow telling the clerk what to say. But the sheriff doesn't. And I don't think old Shorty McGinnis's story is going to change his mind."

"Afraid you're right," Chee said.

Dashee sighed. "You know, Jim, I gotta go down there, anyway. Down to that canyon bottom and see if I can find that old man. Or somebody who knows about him. Or something.

Billy's had too much tough luck. And nobody to help him."

Chee said nothing to that. He'd foreseen it. He knew Cowboy too well to expect any less of him. He took a deep breath.

"Do you think you're going to need some help?"

"Well, I was hoping you'd ask."

"When are you going down there? And how you going? And here's a harder question: How you going to go about this business? Finding a maybe imaginary old man that trades diamonds for things?"

"Sooner the better, is the first answer. And I'm going to make Billy Tuve come along and show me just exactly where he made that trade and try to retrace where the old man he dealt with might have gone in that little bit of time he was gone. What do you think?"

"How many years ago did that happen? Many, many, wasn't it?"

"Billy's always been very vague about chronology. Ever since that horse fell on him."

"So maybe it was ten years, or twenty. Or maybe the old man was out of sight thirty minutes, or thirty hours, or several days?"

"It's not that bad," Dashee said. "He tries."

"So what's plan number two?"

"While Billy and I are looking for the diamond man along the river, I thought you might be mingling among the old folks in the Havasupai settlement. You've had a couple of cases down there. Know some people, don't you? Know a little of their language?"

"Damn little," Chee said. "And all I was doing was looking for stolen property. You don't make friends doing that."

Dashee made a sort of dismissive sound. Or was it just frustration?

"Hell, Jim," he said. "I know it's a long shot. But what am I going to do? Billy's my cousin. It's family. I'm a religious sort of man, you know. So are you. Sometimes we have to just make ourselves an opportunity to get some outside help from the Higher Power. Call it luck, or whatever."

Chee considered that for a while. "How soon you want to do this?"

"Right away, I think. The sheriff sounded like they might be revoking the bond, with that new story they have about the diamond. I thought I'd drive over to Second Mesa in the morning and pick him up before they get the revocation order."

"I'll have to call you back, Cowboy. I'm supposed to get with Bernie tomorrow. You know how it is before a wedding. All sorts of planning stuff."

"So I can't exactly count on you?"

"Well, you probably can. I'll call you."

The telephone rang just after he ended that call. It was Bernie. She'd noticed his number on her "missed calls" tattletale. "What's up?" she said.

"Well," Chee said, "how do I start?"

"You start by telling me you miss me and just wanted to hear the sound of my voice."

"All true, but I also wanted to know what you have planned for us. You were telling me we need to get together. To do some planning." He paused. "And maybe some other things."

Bernie laughed. "Other things are more fun," she said. "But we do have to find a place to live. Unless you're going to change your mind and make that trailer of yours our bridal suite. I hope that wasn't what you were calling to tell me."

"No," Chee said. "But now I've got something else on my mind. Remember Cowboy Dashee's problem?"

"Sort of," Bernie said. "His cousin accused

of shooting that store operator at Zuni, and trying to pawn that big diamond?"

"Well, now it's worse. The store owner's widow and a former clerk at the store are claiming the homicide victim owned the diamond. Dashee thinks the sheriff is going to have the bond revoked, put Tuve back in lockup. Dashee's going down into the canyon. Try to find the old man he claims gave Tuve the diamond. He wants me to go along."

"When?"

"Right away. Like tomorrow."

"Hey," Bernie said. "That sounds like fun. I haven't been down there since I was a teenager."

Chee looked away from the telephone, through the window, at the cloud building over the mountains. Would Bernie ever stop being unpredictable?

"That sounds like you want to go along?"

"Yes, indeed," Bernie said.

"Bernie, going down on a school bus with a bunch of kids won't be anything like this. That must've been some sort of a campground with a road to it. No roads this time. This is going to have to be all the way to the bottom. Climbing down several thousand feet or so. Rough going.

And then we may get stuck down there a day or two, depending on what luck we have finding anything. It's going to be tough."

That produced an extended silence.

Chee said, "Bernie?"

Bernie said, "Jim. I want you to remember. I'm not Officer Bernadette Manuelito, rookie cop, anymore. I resigned from your squad. Now I'm on leave from the U.S. Border Patrol. So I'm not talking to you as Sergeant Chee now. Okay? Now, tell me what makes you think you're any better at climbing down into canyons than I am."

"On leave! I thought you'd resigned."

"Well, I sort of did. But they put me on some sort of medical leave. Sort of let me know I could get my job back if I wanted it."

This was making Jim Chee very nervous.

"Bernie," he said. "I thought . . ."

Bernie was laughing. "I'm sorry," she said. "I was just sort of kidding you, Jim. I'm bad about that. Kidding people. Actually, the only way I'd go back to the Border Patrol would be if I could take you along. And you could be boss, too, since the one I was working for got fired. But first I've got to marry you."

"Sooner the better," Chee said.

"Anyway, I want to go with you. I'll get all

packed, sleeping bag and all. Where are you meeting Cowboy, and when? And do I need to come there, or will you pick me up? I know you have to carry drinking water into the canyon. Should I bring any food?"

Chee sighed. "I guess so," he said, recognizing a lost argument, probably the first of many. But Bernie was right. It would be fun.

10

Brad Chandler had pulled his rental Land Rover into the arriving passengers' parking zone of the Flagstaff airport, scanned those hurrying past to the shuttle buses, and spotted the man who must be the one he had come for. His name was Fred Sherman, a bulky man carrying a bulging briefcase, wearing a sweat-stained cowboy hat, and looking like a middle-aged retired policeman—which was exactly what he was. Chandler lowered the passenger-side window, waved, shouted.

"Hey, Sherman! Over here."

Fred Sherman came to the car, not hurrying. He leaned on the windowsill. "Yo, Chandler," he said. "Long time since I've dealt with you."

Chandler motioned Sherman into the car. "Let's go talk business."

Sherman settled himself in the front seat.

"Pretty fancy truck for a skip tracer to be driving," he said, studying Chandler. "I been wondering what you looked like ever since you got me to help grab that Phoenix bond jumper a while back. You sounded like a kid on the telephone." He chuckled. "Come to think of it, you still did when you called me last week."

"You sounded like some old fart in a nursing home," Chandler said, "but you look healthy enough. What kind of information have you got for me?"

"First I got a question. What's my split on this?"

"No split," Chandler said. "If we bomb out, we pay you your expenses plus your regular hourly rate. If we get the deal done, you get that plus a twenty-thousand bonus."

Sherman digested that. Looked at Chandler. "This don't sound a bit like a bail bond case."

"I already told you that," Chandler said. "I told you I want you to find out everything you can about that robbery-homicide they were holding a Hopi Indian named Billy Tuve for doing. Everything about that big diamond he had that got him arrested. Everything about who has just bonded him out. And why they put up the money. This Tuve hasn't jumped bond. But I want to know where he's living now. Probably he's at his home on the Hopi Reservation. But I want to know for sure. And what's he doing? What's going on? Has he just gone home and rested? Or what?"

It occurred to Chandler as he finished that string of bad-tempered questions that he had adopted exactly the same arrogant tone that Plymale had used with him. Sherman was staring at him now, eyes squinted, an expression that suggested he, Sherman, hadn't liked it any better than Chandler had. But Sherman merely shrugged.

"Well, now," he said. "First I have another question. Where are you taking me now?"

"I'm going to get someplace where those airport security rent-a-cops won't be hassling us to move along. We're going to circle like we're waiting to pick up a passenger. Then when we get our talking done, I'll drop you off at the cabstand."

"It would be quicker to just go into Flagstaff, stop at my hotel, and do our talking in air-conditioned comfort," Sherman said. "Maybe in the bar with a Scotch-and-water in hand."

Chandler ignored that.

Sherman studied him. "I'd guess you have some reason that I can't think of right now not to want somebody or other to see you and me together at the hotel. Does that sound like a sensible guess?"

"Possibly," Chandler said.

"Well, then, let's see if I can answer some of those questions you were asking."

Sherman extracted a slim little notebook from a shirt pocket.

"The bond for Billy Tuve was fifty thou," Sherman began, and recited what else he'd learned at the clerk's office, down to Tuve leaving the place with Joanna Craig.

"Going where?" Chandler asked.

"Be cool," Sherman said. "The hotel where she was staying in Gallup was the El Rancho," he reported, and then rattled off what and who he'd seen there, down to the ordering of room service. "Then . . ."

Sherman paused, peered at Chandler. "I understand this right, don't I? You're paying the expenses."

Chandler nodded.

"I mention it because this cost me twenty bucks. The clerk was getting tired of talking to me. Anyway, then a big, tall Navajo, looked like an athlete, showed up with a Hopi deputy sheriff, asking about Joanna Craig. They went up to her room. A while later another Indian came in.

He said he was supposed to come to the hotel and pick up Billy Tuve. Said he was his uncle giving him a ride back out to Second Mesa, wherever that is. Sounded like he was taking him home. So the clerk called Ms. Craig's room, and they all came out and left."

"All? Tuve left with them? And were they all together? Or how?"

"Tuve left with the man who claimed to be his uncle. Then the other two men left. Don't know about Ms. Craig because I left myself."

"How about why she put up Tuve's bond?"

Sherman responded to that with an incredulous stare.

"Well? What's the answer?"

"If I had been dumb enough to ask her, her answer would have been it was none of my damn business. And who was I, and who was I working for, and so forth," Sherman said. "But I'd guess it's something to do with that lawsuit you were telling me about on the telephone. You didn't tell me much, but you did say we'd be working for one side of some sort of big-money court case."

"How about the diamond? Where it came from?"

"Tuve told the cops an old man swapped it with him for his shovel. Down at the bottom of the Grand Canyon." Sherman laughed. "My connections in the district attorney's office weren't taking that very seriously when I first asked 'em about the case, but I have something new on that. I got a call back from my man there, and he told me—"

"Hold it," Chandler said, and pulled the Land Rover into a tree-shaded turn bay, and stopped. "Told you what?"

"Told me another diamond had turned up. Or at least another diamond story. Come to think of it, two new diamond stories. Both pretty doubtful."

"Go on," Chandler said.

"This first one sounds like what you call a groundless rumor. My man heard from a cop he knows in the New Mexico State Police, got it from somebody in the Navajo County Sheriff's Department, who picked it up in Window Rock. Probably from Navajo Tribal Police, who—"

"Come on," said Chandler. "Cut down on the BS. What's the story?"

Sherman said nothing.

Chandler glanced at him, noticed his expression. Said, "Sorry. I didn't mean to sound so impatient."

"The story is that a little trading post at

Short Mountain, way up in the northwest corner of the Navajo Reservation, got burglarized some years back. Owner gave the cops a list of missing stuff, including a very expensive diamond. When this robbery-homicide Tuve pulled off came up, with Tuve trying to pawn a big diamond, the old Navajo cop who had worked the Short Mountain case checked on it. The trader claimed a cowboy had come in out of a snowstorm and traded it to him for some groceries and a ride into Page. This cowboy said he was down at the bottom of the Grand Canyon and an old man came along and swapped him the diamond for a fancy jackknife he had."

Chandler considered this without comment.

"End of story," Sherman said. "You ready to have me hurry through the other one?"

"You have the name of the Navajo cop who checked into this? Or the trading post owner? Or whether this diamond swap was in the same part of the canyon? That damned Grand Canyon is two hundred and seventy-seven miles long and more than ten miles wide."

"It couldn't be as long as that," Sherman said. "And I don't know where he got the diamond. Don't know the names, either. But I guess I can get them."

"I'll want them," Chandler said. "Now, what's the other story?"

"Exactly what you'd expect. The widow of the guy killed in that curio store robbery claims Tuve lied in his story about where he got that stone. She said her husband had that big diamond for years and she wanted to make damn sure the law took good care of it and gave it back to her when the trial was over."

Chandler laughed.

Sherman grinned at him. "I didn't really think that would surprise you."

"It doesn't," Chandler said. "I think I may have gotten myself involved in a situation in which diamonds have punched the avarice button on two greedy women."

"Two? Who's the other one? You mean that Craig woman? How does she fit in?"

Sherman was leaning back against the passenger-side door, studying Chandler, watching a driver who had hoped to use the turnout lane creeping cautiously past.

Chandler ignored the question.

"I think you need to tell me what this is all about," Sherman said. "Otherwise I might run across something useful and not even know it."

"Like what?"

"Well, hell. Like who we're trying to find. He might walk right past me."

Chandler laughed. "I don't think that's likely. This guy who is being looked for is dead."

"Dead?"

"And we're not trying to find him. Or if we do, we'll never admit it. We'll just hide him again."

Sherman, not enjoying this, said, "I don't like playing children's guessing games. What are you paying me to do?"

Chandler took a folded envelope out of his shirt pocket.

"There's a list of stuff in here. Where you can find me, phone number, all that. And a list of instructions. Information I need. Names. All that. Then I want you to locate Tuve, find that woman who posted bond for him. If she went back to where she came from, find her address and what she does there. If she stayed out here, find out where and what she's doing. Who she's talking to, all that."

Sherman took the envelope, extracted the note inside, read it, stared at Chandler.

"I'll still say I could be a lot more useful, and quicker, if I know what our goal is in all this."

Chandler nodded. He gave Sherman a quick

summary starting with the airlines colliding, then moving on to the diamond case padlocked to the arm. But how much of this did he want Sherman to know?

"It was a man named Clarke," he continued. "Like most of the victims, his body was never recovered."

Sherman was frowning. "You going to tell me we're looking for this Clarke bird? Dead for how many years?"

"No. I was going to tell you that a daughter of his old girlfriend got a psychic message through some spiritualist that Clarke had his arm torn off in the crash, and he sent her psychic orders to find it and bury it properly with the rest of his corpse so it would quit hurting him in the spirit world."

"Come on," Sherman said. "Get serious." He laughed.

"The one she wants is the arm that had the case of diamonds handcuffed to it."

Sherman considered that for a moment, said, "Oh, I guess I get the picture."

"I'm not quite certain I get it myself. But it seems like the interests you and me are representing here are the foundation which inherited all that Clarke fortune. And probably the insurance, which paid out its hundred thousand dollars maximum airline flight fee for the jewels, and somebody interested in patching Clarke's body back together."

"And you figure that burial sentiment is actually based on trying to get those diamonds, right?"

"Well, a civil suit is now hung up in court. A woman is claiming to be an out-of-wedlock granddaughter of Old Man Clarke and therefore the valid heiress to the Clarke billions. And that lawsuit was months after the news that even old bones can yield DNA evidence to prove family lineage."

"I've heard about that crash, I think," Sherman said. "Long, long time ago, wasn't it? And we're trying to find the bones of that guy carrying the diamonds." He shook his head, laughed. "You serious?"

"Well, actually it's not that simple. Here we have one side of a two-sided game. People on the other side are trying to find those bones and use them to capture the Clarke fortune," Chandler said. "Our job is to make sure that poor fellow's bones stay lost and never get dragged into a courtroom."

Sherman considered that, face solemn. Then

he smiled. "Yeah," he said. "That sounds like a worthy cause with righteous purposes. And I can see how that would be a lot easier."

Chandler nodded.

"Finding old bones down in that canyon is worse than hunting the needle in the haystack. It's like hunting the needle in a whole farm full of haystacks. And not even knowing which farm it's on. So maybe we could just be happy with keeping anyone else from finding them."

"Yes," Chandler said. "Easier to find the hunter than the needle."

"You sound like maybe you have a plan," Sherman said. "I'd like to hear it. You know, it helps me if I understand what you're trying to do."

"You're getting the idea now," Chandler said. "First, we understand our goal. Our goal is not—underline that, **not**—not to find the bones. Our goal is to keep somebody else from finding them. We want to find 'em, that's good, but only because then we can make sure the other folks don't get their hands on them. You understand that?"

"Sure," Sherman said, looking slightly resentful. "I already said I understood it."

"That's the first thing to understand. Now,

the second thing is this. We know that case full of diamonds was handcuffed to the owner's arm. To the bones in question. We have to presume that the Tuve diamond, and that trading post burglary diamond, came from that package. Thus they are the only clues to where those bones might be. The other side, the bad guys, know as much about that as we do. Maybe more. So our goal is to get there first. Got it?"

"Of course," he said, and then thought about it awhile. "Then do what? My impression is that your paycheck depends on the other side never getting hold of those bones. At least not long enough to get them into court. Right? So what do we do if the other side gets there first?"

"I guess that would depend on how much you wanted to earn that big bonus," Chandler said. "I guess you'd do whatever the situation demanded. You know. To get those bones away from the bad guys."

Sherman spent another moment thinking.

"Arizona is a death penalty state," he said. "For murder done in commission of a felony, anyway. But I'll bet you already knew that."

"I did," Chandler agreed. "I also know the bottom of that canyon is loaded with dangerous places. Falling rocks. Folks swept away in the river rapids. Drowning. People slipping and tumbling down the cliffs."

Sherman nodded. Grinned at Chandler. "Wouldn't you hate to be the district attorney trying to prove somebody was pushed instead of just slipped? I mean, when nobody saw what happened?"

"Sounds like a case of reasonable doubt to me," Chandler said. "Okay, then. Here's what I want you to do. And the very first thing, right now, today, is locate Billy Tuve."

"Any idea where?"

"He lives on Second Mesa. You heard his uncle saying he'd come to take him home. He lives with his mama in a little village. Kykotsmovi, however you pronounce it. Shouldn't be hard to find it."

"Find him and what?"

"Find him and bring him to me."

"Then what?"

"Then we take him down to the bottom of the canyon, to the area where he got the diamond. Then he shows us how to find where the man he got it from came from. When we find that man, then we find the left arm bones of this Clarke guy and what's left of the diamonds he was carrying."

"And split them?"

"Well, I presume the man who's hiring us would want them himself. But I don't think he has them counted."

Sherman laughed. "He wouldn't miss a few of 'em."

11

The plan, carefully drawn up by Sergeant Jim Chee, involved having Bernie spend the evening with him at his Shiprock trailer, during which they would enjoy themselves and pack up the assorted stuff they needed for the junket into the depth of the Grand Canyon. Then they would head westward to Tuba City. Meanwhile, Cowboy Dashee would have gone to Kykotsmovi on the Hopi Second Mesa and picked up Billy Tuve at his family home there. That done, Dashee would bring Tuve to the grocery store/service station at Tuba, where they'd meet Chee and Bernie. From there, Cowboy would lead the way on a back-road shortcut to Moenkopi, thence westward via an unimproved and unnamed dirt road to a place on the East Rim just north of the Little Colorado Canyon gorge. They would park there. Dashee and Tuve, both members of the prestigious Hopi Bear Clan and thus both Salt Trail initiates, would lead them down, down, down into the depths. Once at the bottom, Tuve would show them exactly where he had traded his folding shovel for the diamond, and the direction he'd seen the owner of the gem take to retrieve it.

As such careful and detailed plans tend to do, this one began falling apart in phase one.

"I'm not going to drive all the way to Shiprock this afternoon to spend the night with you, Mr. Chee, in that old trailer," said Bernadette Manuelito. "I have to get my stuff together. Get my boots, and hiking stuff, sleeping bag, all that. You have to meet Dashee anyway. Can't you pick me up on the way? I'll meet you over at Yah-ta-hey. At the trading post."

Chee sighed. "We're meeting Dashee at Tuba City at five A.M.," he said. "So I guess we could meet at Yah-ta-hey. But we'd have to leave Yah-ta-hey about three A.M., I'd say. Can you handle getting up that early?"

"Hey, man," Bernie said. "You're forgetting I've been a Border Patrolman."

Indeed, Bernie seemed wide awake as well as loaded with water bottles, foodstuff, and luggage when he pulled up at Yah-ta-hey. However, after a hundred miles and a lot of talking of wedding plans, snuggling, and so forth, they saw no sign of Dashee or Billy Tuve at their Tuba City meeting place. Chee looked at his watch and grumbled. "When I'm late, Cowboy always gives me that 'Navajo time' complaint," he said. "As if the Hopis were perfect."

"If I were you I'd just call him. Find out what happened."

Chee extracted his cell phone, dialed Dashee's cell number, let it ring, heard Dashee's voice.

"Is this Chee?" Dashee said. "I was just going to call you. Tuve's gone."

It wasn't a good connection.

"Tuve's what? Gone where?"

"When I got to his place, his mother was there. She said a car drove up yesterday about suppertime. She was out seeing about the sheep, but she saw Billy out in front talking to somebody. When she got back to the house, the car was driving away. She went on in, looking for Billy, but he was gone."

Chee considered that. Said, "What do you think?"

"Now I don't know what to think," Dashee

said. "But then I told Billy's mother maybe the sheriff had come to get him. Needed some more information from him. Or maybe the bail bond business had been canceled."

"That sounds reasonable," Chee said.

"Sure does, but it wasn't. On the way down off Second Mesa I met a McKinley County Sheriff's car going up the slope. Flagged him down. He said he was going out to Tuve's place to pick him up. Said more evidence had come in and Tuve's bail had been revoked."

"This is interesting," Chee said. "So what do you think happened to him?"

"I don't have a clue. It doesn't seem to make any sense. But I've got an idea."

Bernie tapped Chee on the arm, said, "What's interesting, and who is the 'him' that something happened to? Was it Billy Tuve?"

Cowboy was talking into Chee's other ear.

"Hold it a second, Cowboy. I'll bring Bernie up to date on this."

"My idea," said Cowboy, "is that Craig woman who bailed him out came and got him. Remember, she wanted him to take her down into the canyon. Show her where he got the diamond."

"I remember," Chee said. "But I also remember he told her he wouldn't do it. And then she said, well, she'd go anyway. Or something like that."

"What's he telling you?" Bernie asked.

"Shut up a minute, will you, Cowboy?" Chee said. He put the phone on his lap, told Bernie what Cowboy had told him, and reclaimed the telephone.

"Well, anyway, I don't have any better ideas. Where are you? And what do we do now?"

Cowboy, it developed, was just rolling over the hump on 264 and dropping down into the Moenkopi draw. "I'll be with you there in Tuba in about twenty minutes."

And he was. As Chee had suggested, he parked his pickup in the Tuba City police station lot. Then he climbed out, took off his hat, nodded to Bernie and Chee.

"Well," he said. "As Jim was just asking us, what do we do now?"

12

Joe Leaphorn was listening to the coffee perking and deciding whether he would double his fried egg ration this morning and cut back on other food later in the day. His rationale for that indulgence was having slept later than usual this morning, having been up past eleven the night before on the phone with Louisa. It had been a long conversation, starting with her report on her interview with the old lady at the Havasupai settlement. He had responded with his own report on his Shorty McGinnis encounter, and McGinnis's tale of trading the cowboy for a diamond. That had triggered a bunch of questions, most of which he couldn't answer, and that had led backward into the whole business of Cowboy Dashee's cousin Billy Tuve, the problem he'd brought crashing down on himself by trying to pawn such a diamond, and Jim Chee's involvement in the whole Billy Tuve mess.

"When did Tuve get it?" Louisa had asked.

"Several years ago is about the best I can tell you. Tuve's very vague on chronology. He did some rodeo riding, and his horse fell on him, and he suffered some brain damage."

"I've always thought rodeo riders are brain damaged before they get on the horse," Louisa said. "But how about the other man? I mean McGinnis's cowboy. The one who swapped his folding shovel for the diamond. Do you have any specific date when that happened?"

"Well, the burglary in which Shorty claimed the thing was stolen was twelve years ago, but Shorty said he couldn't remember how many years he'd had the diamond before that. I think he said 'several.' I guess it would be about the same with Billy Tuve."

"Except with Tuve, I guess we could find out the year he went down that Hopi Salt Trail for his Bear Clan initiation rite."

"Good idea," Leaphorn said. Why hadn't he thought of that? Probably because he was retired. It was none of his business. "But why is the timing important?"

"Well, it probably isn't," Louisa said. "But it helps me understand what I've been hearing down here in the canyon. Both of these old people I've been trying to collect origin stories from are full of tales of some huge airplane disaster that happened when they were young. Bodies falling out of the sky. Fires in the canyons. All sort of stuff raining down. Clothing. Suitcases. Dishes. Everything. The Park Service people here tell me it happened in 1956, two airlines collided over the canyon. Everybody killed."

"Does seem to be the sort of thing that might produce some new legends," Leaphorn said.

"Or get mixed in with the original ones," Louisa said. "That's my worry. I'm already noticing a mixing of the stories of the various Yuman tribes you have around here with what must have been seen in that disaster. Mixing was already a problem. The Hualapai, the Supai, and some Mohave branches, and even Paiutes—even the Utes and the Paiutes are borrowing bits and pieces of legends from each other. Now we find them mixing in stories about stuff being found."

Leaphorn's interest abruptly sharpened. "Are you hearing things about diamonds?"

"Not specifically, but lots about the stuff found when people were out helping the rescue crews locate missing parts of bodies and airplane parts. And there's one about a Hualapai man from Peach Springs who came down to the river to see what was going on and saw something that might be diamond-connected. The way the most common version of that story goes, he saw some clothing items, or something, caught in a drift of debris, and in this pile of jetsam he saw a human arm." Louisa paused a moment for Leaphorn's reaction to that. Got none. "Is there some reason that doesn't surprise you?"

"Couple of reasons," Leaphorn said. "Body parts were scattered all over in that crash— across the mesa top, down the canyon walls, down into the river itself. Rescue crews were collecting body bits in bags. And besides, I heard the arm story before."

"Did the arm you're hearing about have some sort of attaché case connected to it? Maybe with a chain and a handcuff?"

"Yep," Leaphorn said. "That's the one. But the man who spotted it in my story couldn't reach it without drowning. When he got back with some helpers, the river had swept it away. Long ago, of course. I would have thought it would be pretty well forgotten by now."

Louisa laughed. "Joe! Who's going to forget

seeing an arm sticking out of debris in their river? That's good enough to make a Greek myth. It's one of the problems for us seekers of undiluted, genuine legends, ancient and uninfected by our unromantic modern times."

"I guess you're right."

"Besides, if that arm with the case chained to it had been forgotten, somebody has stirred it up again."

"How?" Leaphorn asked. "And who? And why would they?"

"They printed a sheet offering a ten-thousand-dollar reward for just such a set of arm bones. Someone distributed them at the Grand Canyon Hotel, the private one, and at the National Park Service hotel, and visitor centers, and got them spread around among the professional guide and float trip outfits, and at Peach Springs. There's a number to call—I think it's in Flagstaff—if you find the arm and want to collect." Louisa laughed. "I should have saved one for you."

"Get one for me if you can, Louisa. What did it say?"

"Well, a big headline across the top said 'Ten-Thousand-Dollar Reward.' And under that—in smaller type—it said something like 'Family of

1956 airline crash victim seeks bones of the left arm of John Clarke, so that they can be placed with his body in the family's burial crypt.' And then it went on to explain the arm had been torn from his body when those two airlines collided over the canyon and had never been recovered. It said the bones could be identified because the forearm had been broken previously and repaired with a surgical pin when this Clarke was young, or the forearm might still be attached by a metal and cuff to which a leather case was secured."

"I'd really like to have a couple of those flyers," Leaphorn said. "One for Jim Chee. I think he and Dashee are going to take Tuve down in the canyon and try to find the man he got the diamond from."

That produced a long pause.

"After God knows how many years?" Louisa said. "How in the world are they going to find him? No name or anything. That sounds impossible."

"Yeah," Leaphorn said. "All they know is where the swap was made and that the old fellow with the diamonds was an Indian, but not a Hopi or Navajo, and after the swap deal was agreed on, he had to go down the canyon maybe a half-mile to get the stone. Their guess is he must have been some sort of hermit—maybe a Havasupai shaman—who had the diamonds cached in a cave."

"What's your guess?"

"My guess is they won't find anyone, but you know them both. Jim will feel better because he did what he could to help his old friend, and Cowboy will rest easier because he did his duty to his family and his fellow Bear Clan member."

Louisa sighed. "Sure," she said. "You'd do the same thing, wouldn't you?"

Before he could think of an honest answer to that, Louisa had something to add.

"Hermit, you said. That old woman I talked to yesterday was telling about the last shaman they had—he died back in the 1960s, I think it was—and how a man from the Kaibab Paiute Reservation was a friend of the shaman and was always hanging around Peach Springs. From what she told me, he was living on a sort of part-time basis with a Havasupai woman. She said he was a 'far-looking man,' the Supai name for people who can see into the future, find things, all that. Sort of like your Navajo crystal-gazer shaman. Anyway, he got into some sort of trouble and left Peach Springs and went away somewhere and disappeared. Supposed to have made himself some sort of nest in one of those undercut places up a side canyon and was living off crawdads, frogs, and stuff he could get off of the tourist rafters who are always floating down the river through there. She said people sometimes crossed the river there to learn things from him. Get him to take a peek into the distant future for them."

"Hmmm," Leaphorn said.

Louisa laughed. "Too bad they didn't ask him how to find those diamonds you and Chee seem so interested in. My source at Peach Springs said he seemed to do a lot of business with people after that airplane disaster. Lots of lost things to be found."

"Yeah," Leaphorn said. "Such as friends and relatives. And including a torn-off left arm with a package of diamonds attached."

"I could bring you a couple copies of that flier," Louisa said. "But if you need it faster, I heard whoever did it ran the same message as little advertisements in the **Navajo News,** and the Flagstaff paper, and other papers around there. Easy to find out and easy to get a copy."

"Really?" Leaphorn said. He was thinking of how much it must have cost to get all this printing and advertising done, thinking about what Captain Pinto had said, of Pinto's speculation about the importance Washington was putting on the federal part of this peculiar situation. He was thinking this was getting much more interesting.

"Joe? You still there?"

"Can you do me a favor, Louisa? Could you find out everything you can learn about this possible hermit? His name? Is he still alive? Did he stay on the Peach Springs side of the river? Does anyone know where he might be? Anyway, just let me know anything you can find out about him."

"Okay, Joe. But if I do, you're going to have to promise me you'll keep me informed. I don't want to read about something spectacular in the **Farmington Times** or the **Gallup Independent**."

"Okay," Leaphorn said. "I promise."

"One other thing you might be interested in. Among the various new legends and revisions of old ones that disaster spread around is a renewed interest in Masaw. You remember him?"

"The Hopi kachina spirit who is a sort of guardian of this world. The one who greeted them when they came up out of the fourth world, and told them where to live, and not to be afraid of death. Masaw, or Skeleton Man, or Maasau'u, or—"

"Or two or three other names," Louisa said. "Anyway some old man, maybe that hermit I mentioned, was supposed to be trying to start a sort of Skeleton Man sect. To get people to quit being so obsessed with having those one hundred and twenty-eight bodies showering down on them."

"Sort of like all that therapy business in Colorado after all those kids got shot at the school, I guess," Leaphorn said.

"Sort of," Louisa agreed. "And listen, if Chee and Officer Dashee are coming down here, let me know where I can find them. Cell phones are pretty chancy, but sometimes they work. I'm talking to you on mine right now."

"Fair enough," Leaphorn said. "And when you're back here, I want to show you the little leather pollen pouch that the diamond Shorty McGinnis showed me had been kept in. It has an animal-looking symbol sewed into it. New to me but I thought you might recognize it."

"These days it would probably be something out of a Disney movie," Louisa said.

After they clicked off, it occurred to him that

he hadn't told Louisa where to find Chee or Dashee. In fact, he didn't know himself.

Where had he jotted down that cell phone number? Back of an envelope maybe. He'd sort through his wastebasket. Hope to get lucky. Or call the NTP office at Shiprock. Maybe someone there would have it.

13

Joanna Craig had followed Tuve on his homeward trip. His uncle had put him into a very dusty and much-dented pickup. Pickup trucks in Indian country are as common as taxicabs in Manhattan, but this one helped Joanna's cause by carrying in its bed a huge box, big enough to house a king-sized refrigerator, with a gaudy red Kitchen Aide label.

A couple of times she'd needed the help. Tuve's uncle had ducked into a service station at Ganado, and she would have lost him had she not seen the big box sticking up as she rolled past on the highway. She would have lost him again just past the Polacca settlement when he made a turn she hadn't anticipated, and then been lured into following another pickup, same shade of blue, same degree of dustiness. But she

had again spotted the Kitchen Aide advertise-
ment, did an illegal U-turn across the highway,
and followed the box up a narrow road that
struggled up the slopes of First Mesa to serve the
little stone villages of Walpi, Hano, and Si-
chomovi and whatever lay beyond them.

And now there it was, box and truck, parked
down a short stretch of weedy track that led to a
flat stone house and its supporting storage shed,
sheep pen, outhouse, and the rusty remains of an
earlier pickup. She saw no sign of Tuve, his uncle, or anyone else, and drove past. She found a
cluster of junipers where she could park mostly
out of sight and watch the house. She would
wait, and worry, and reconsider her strategy for
doing what she absolutely had to do, must do,
was destined to do. Usually she thought of it as
getting justice. When she was angry, she admitted her goal was revenge, but now that she was
here, she knew it was fate. Fate had moved her
along. This was the only way she could destroy
Dan Plymale. And that was her dream and her
destiny.

No need for the car's air conditioner in the
cool, dry air of the Hopi Mesa. She rolled down
the window, got her binoculars out of the glove

box, and focused on the Tuve home place. The truck was empty. Nothing stirred but a faint plume of smoke that came from the horno oven behind the house. She had already considered and rejected the idea of simply knocking on the door, introducing herself, and explaining to Tuve's mother and uncle why she had put up bail for Billy Tuve and why she desperately needed his help. She was certain she could sway Billy—had seen the sympathy showing in his face in her hotel room. But mother and uncle were older, would be skeptical, would be more religious, would be impossible to persuade that the Salt Trail rules could be bent. She'd have to wait for an opportunity to get Billy alone. At least wait until after his uncle had left. Without someone there to interrupt her, Joanna was sure she could use that combination of his own self-interest and his sympathy for her own plight to persuade him. And probably his mother, too.

Whether Tuve could find the man who supplied him his trouble-making gem seemed less likely, and even if he did, whether that would lead her to her father's bones was another unanswerable question. But she would recover those bones. And they would prove she was heir to the

Clarke fortune and bring Dan Plymale and his phony, greed-driven Eternal Peace Foundation crashing down in bankrupt ruins.

Someone had emerged from the rear of the Tuve house. She shifted to the passenger window, getting a clearer view, and focused on a woman, plump, walking slowly, carrying a basket to a clothesline strung between the storage shed and a nearby tree, hanging out a shirt, a pair of denims, socks, underwear. Probably what Tuve had been wearing when he was taken to jail.

Joanna dropped the binoculars on the seat and squirmed into a more comfortable position. Ready for more waiting, more planning, more remembering. And for reinforcing the absolute confidence she must have to finish this job. She would because she must. Because it was her fate. Fate had been painfully slow, but it had finally led her here, and it would take her to those bones, and they would give her—finally—the peace of knowing she had done her duty. The peace of taking on her own name, of having it legally changed to Joanna Clarke. Having finally revenged her mother. And her father. And herself.

Revenge had been her purpose since she was in high school, living with her mother and her mother's elderly husband in his lavish summer home in the Montana mountains, and finally learning that Craig was a fiction and that her father was John Clarke.

The elderly husband had been dying of some variation of cancer, probably had been dying when her mother, just thirty at the time, married him, an old gray man with a chauffeur-driven car. Joanna had been a flower girl at the wedding, only nine but old enough even then to wonder why her mother was the bride of a frail-looking grandfather. It wasn't until her mother's death the year after she'd graduated from the University of Montana that she knew the rest of the story. Or knew her real name.

Her mother's lawyer had given her the letter—a thick envelope with a stamped wax seal. On it her mother had written: "To be given to my daughter, Joanna Clarke, in the event of my death."

A man emerged from the front door of the Tuve house. Joanna refocused the binoculars. Tuve's uncle, with Tuve standing in the open door saying something to him. Uncle climbed into the pickup, the motor started, the truck backed down the track, turned on to the road, and headed slowly down the way they had come.

Billy Tuve disappeared from the doorway, closed the door. Joanna switched her view to the back of the house, located Tuve's mother at the sheep pen, the gate open now, the sheep emerging. Joanna turned her view to the pickup, disappearing now over the mesa rim. Back to Tuve's mother. She was following the sheep, presumably to where they would be grazing. The front door was still closed. She would wait about five minutes. Then she would call on Billy Tuve, and persuade him, and take him to the top of the Salt Trail, and down it to realize her destiny.

Destiny, however, did not allow her a full five minutes. Just as she turned the ignition key to start the engine to drive down to Tuve's house, to complete this phase of her project, another car emerged over the rim, a white sedan moving fast. Joanna decided she would wait another minute to allow it to pass. It didn't. It slowed, turned down the track to the Tuve house, stopped there. A man emerged, a big man. Billy Tuve appeared at the front door. They met in the doorway and talked. To Joanna, her binoculars focused, they appeared to be arguing. Billy made a negative gesture. The argument resumed. Billy disappeared inside. The man waited on the doorstep. And waited.

Joanna glanced at her watch. Two minutes passed. Four minutes. The man leaned against the door frame, shifted his hat to shade his face from the sun.

Joanna suddenly felt sick. She knew who this man must be. He would be a man named Sherman. The man who had been at the Park Service Center just before her, asking questions about where victims of that plane crash were buried, and then asking about who had been handing out the sheets offering a reward for information about them.

"You just missed him," the clerk had told her. "He was really curious about your reward offer. He said his name was Sherman and he needed to find you. I asked him if he knew anything about the diamonds and he just laughed."

The name Sherman might be phony, Joanna thought, but whatever it was, it might as well be Plymale. He'd be bought and paid by that lawyer, just one of the tentacles answering to Dan Plymale. Which meant Plymale had got to Billy Tuve before her.

As she thought that, Billy Tuve reappeared in the doorway. He was carrying a zippered bag of blue canvas which seemed fairly heavy as he swung it into the back seat of Sherman's car.

They drove away down the mesa road and over the rim.

Joanna, feeling sick and shaken, followed. Following was easier this time because she was almost sure she knew where they were going and the vehicle was an easy-to-spot white sedan. But what would she have to do when they got there? She pulled her purse over beside her, snapped it open, reached inside, extracted a pistol, and steeled herself for what lay ahead.

The pistol, like most everything she was doing, as well as her fierce malice, her nightmare dreams, dated back to the letter her mother had left her. She could remember it, word for word.

Dearest Joanna:

I have lied to you all these years because I didn't want you to inherit the pain I have lived through since your father died. But I believe you must know. Lieutenant David Shaw, killed in Vietnam after your conception, was a lie. He didn't exist. He was my cover story. Your father was John Clarke Jr., killed in that awful airliner collision in Arizona about six months before your birth. He was

**flying home for our wedding. His
father (your grandfather, although he
never would have admitted it) was a
widower. He had already told John, his
only child, that he would not attend
the ceremony. He told me in a letter
that I was "gold-digging white trash, in
no way fit for his family."**

Much of the rest of that first page recounted
other such insults. It told how the elder Clarke,
already the victim of two heart attacks, had suffered a stroke during those days when the hunt
was on for the bodies of airline crash victims. He
died without recovering from the coma and his
affairs were taken over by his law firm, the Plymale firm, which represented a tax-exempt foundation the old man had started.

The law firm was Plymale, Stevens, Eber-
sten, and Daly, and one of its junior members
was Dan Plymale Jr., son of the senior partner.
The firm seemed to have suspected that Joanna's
mother had conceived young Clarke's child. The
senior Plymale contacted her, told her she had
no claim to any share of the estate, but offered
her ten thousand dollars to sign a legal dis-
claimer. She had discussed this with Hal Sim-

mons, who told her that the senior Clarke's will left the bulk of his estate to John, or descendants of John if John preceded him in death. If no such descendants existed, the bulk of the estate went to the foundation he had initiated with the guidance of Dan Plymale. The executor of the estate, and the director of the charity foundation, was to be Plymale's law firm.

She had given Hal Simmons copies of the love letters John had written her, including those discussing her pregnancy, along with the final letter. In that, Clarke said he would be "home tomorrow to hold you in my arms, and take you down to the church and thereby make that little child we have conceived legal and respectable— and to hell with what Daddy Clarke thinks of it."

Simmons met with the Plymales, father and son. He showed them the letters and proposed a negotiated settlement. The Plymales refused, saying the letters were not sufficient evidence. However, in view of the pregnancy, they offered to increase the ten-thousand-dollar settlement offer to thirty thousand dollars, providing that the fetus would be aborted, and proof of the abortion provided.

Joanna remembered precisely what her mother had written: "Remember, Joanna, the twenty thousand dollars they added to the offer. That was the value they put on your life. Twenty thousand dollars the fee for killing you in my womb."

Twenty thousand dollars! When she heard that was the estimated value of her father's diamond, the diamond poor Billy Tuve had tried to pawn for twenty dollars, the irony struck deep. She had laughed and then she'd cried, and then she'd wondered if that had been the very diamond her father had been bringing home to her mother as a wedding gift, and then she had cried again. And now it turned out to be that this diamond, or another one just like it, was leading her to her destiny.

Simmons told her mother that the Plymales probably had the right reading of the laws. They would need more evidence to prove that her unborn child was the product of Clarke's seed. With some of the money her mother had inherited from her husband's estate and perhaps the promise of a generous contingency agreement, Simmons retained a national private investigation firm to learn everything possible about John Clarke, his jewelry business, the last months of his life, and the circumstances of his death.

The information had come in slowly. First

the knowledge that her father had been bringing a package of specially cut diamonds back to New York from Los Angeles. That information had come from a dealer in Manhattan's diamond district who had been awaiting them. Seventy-four stones, ranging in weight from 3.7 carats to 7.2, all of them perfect blue-whites, one specially cut for her mother—just as John Clarke had told her in his terminal letter. And in that final letter, her father had drawn a neat little sketch of the gem, showing how the cutter had shaped it for her.

From airline employees in Los Angeles, the agency collected statements confirming that Clarke had boarded the aircraft with the diamond case locked to his left wrist, and that he had fended off security people who wanted to open it for inspection, explaining that those carrying diamonds—like security messengers—couldn't unlock such cases. The key to do that had been delivered by another messenger to the person who would receive them, count them, weigh them, and sign receipts for them.

From National Park Service employees, guides who worked in the canyon, from Arizona police, from a half-dozen Havasupai citizens who had been involved in recovering bodies and parts of the shattered aircraft, the agency learned that

Clarke's body had not been recovered for identification. They also learned that one of a party of tourists who had been on a guided raft float down the Colorado eleven days after the disaster had seen a body part, a forearm, in driftwood debris below one of the rapids. He had not been able to reach the driftwood through the current but had taken photographs from a nearby outcrop. When a party of guides managed to be back there two weeks later to recover the arm, it was gone, as was part of the collected flotsam the man had seen with it. A search downstream proved fruitless.

The agency reported that the man who shot the photographs was now dead but his family had kept prints and negatives as a sort of macabre souvenir of what had been, at the time, the worst airline disaster in history. Copies were made and provided to Simmons and her mother, and now Joanna kept copies in her purse. They were the only photographs she had of her father. The Clarke family relatives had refused her requests for old family pictures.

In the final report, the agency provided a collection of interviews with a number of people—mostly Havasupai, some Grand Canyon National Park employees, some professional guides, some tourists passing through—who spoke of reports about a man, described generally as having long gray or white hair, being slender, wearing worn or ragged clothing, having claimed to have found a severed arm in the Colorado River, or recovered it from a drift of flotsam. While these stories varied in many details, most of those interviewed agreed that the man had been on what is called the "south side" of the river—below the most tourist-popular South Rim—and downstream from where the Little Colorado River Canyon connects to the Grand Canyon. They also seemed in various ways to suggest that he was a hermit, some sort of eccentric, perhaps a religious fanatic. Two of these proposed that he was a Havasupai shaman who had disappeared about twenty years earlier and was remembered as a visionary with a talent for finding lost children, missing animals, anything lost.

The way Joanna saw it, an important element of these fragmentary "hermit reports" was the mention in three of them that this strange fellow had considered himself either a priest or the guardian of a shrine. One report included his description of what happened when sunlight reached this shrine: "He said when this happened it 'responded to the Father Sun with a dazzling light,' but he said this occurred only late in the morning with the sun almost overhead."

To Joanna, "dazzling light" suggested the sun striking diamonds, which perhaps decorated this odd man's shrine. But more important was the dating of these third-hand reports. In one the person being interviewed said he had met this hermit only three years earlier. Another had placed his conversation with the man "probably about July, two years back."

Thus it was reasonable to think he was still alive. And the man who could help her find this hermit was just ahead. The white sedan was slowing, turning down tracks that led to the rim of the mesa, led to the edge of the long, long drop down into the canyon. Probably led to the starting point of the Hopi trail that headed down to the Salt Shrine.

Joanna stopped at the turnoff point, watched and waited until the white sedan disappeared behind a screen of junipers. Then she followed slowly. Give them just enough time to get their bottom-of-the-canyon gear out of the car. Her plan was to get there just before they started their descent. What then? She would decide when she had to.

But there was the white sedan, parked. The two men still in it. The passenger-side door opened, was jerked closed again. Joanna parked, snatched up her binoculars, and stared. Some sort of struggle seemed to be going on. Then it ended. She could make out what must be Tuve's head against the passenger-side window, and part of the driver's face. He was talking.

Joanna got out, holding her pistol behind her. She walked slowly to the rear of the white sedan, keeping to the driver's side, keeping out of the line of sight of the man she presumed was Sherman, glad for the silence of the hiking shoes she was wearing. She could hear his voice now through the open car window, loud and angry. She slid along against the side of the sedan now, seeing Billy Tuve huddled against the opposite door, face down.

Sherman was moving his right hand up and down, a gesture of some sort. He was staring at Tuve, still talking. The right hand held a pistol. Joanna looked down at her own pistol, smaller than the police model Sherman was waving. She cocked it, made certain the safety was off. Very quietly she took the required two more steps, stood at the open car window, thrust her pistol through it, pressed the muzzle against Sherman's neck, said, "Mr. Sherman, drop that pistol on your lap."

"What?" Sherman said, in a strangled voice. He tried to turn his head.

Joanna jammed her pistol under his ear, said, "Drop it. Now. Or die."

Sherman dropped his pistol. Said, "I'm police. Who the hell are you? Let me get my badge out."

"Take that pistol of yours by the end of the barrel with your left hand," Joanna said, keeping the pressure of her gun against his ear. "Then reach around and hand it to me. Butt first. Otherwise I pull the trigger and you've got a bullet in your head."

"Be cool," Sherman said. "Be easy." He reached over with his left hand, took the pistol barrel between thumb and first finger, and handed it back to her—butt first.

Joanna had reached her own left hand into her jacket pocket and extracted a dainty little handkerchief. With that she accepted Sherman's pistol, glanced at it, noticed it wasn't cocked.

"I know who you are," Sherman said. "You're that woman who's trying to get her hands on that big Clarke estate," he said. "Or maybe you're someone working for her."

"And you are a private eye named Sherman," Joanna said. "What are you doing here?"

"He was going to kill me," Billy Tuve said. He had turned and sat facing her, back pressed against his door. "He said if I didn't take him down our Salt Trail, he'd shoot me and throw me over the edge and let the coyotes eat me."

"Little bastard's lying," Sherman said. "He promised me. I wasn't going to shoot him."

"Tell me who you're working for," Joanna said. "I already know, but I want to confirm it. So don't lie."

Sherman was facing her now, looking into the muzzle of her pistol, held just too far from him to reach if he decided to try.

"His name's Chandler," the man said. "Bradford Chandler. Runs Skippers Agency, I think it is." Joanna considered this. "Chandler hired you," she said. "Who hired him? And what's he supposed to do?"

Sherman made a face, bit his lower lip, considered. "You probably already know about the lost jewelry," he said.

"Keep talking."

"Chandler wants it."

Joanna nodded. Said, "And . . ."

Sherman shrugged. "You think there's more to it than that?"

"I know there's more to it than that. You already mentioned the estate. But you haven't told me who hired this Bradford Chandler."

"Look," Sherman said, his voice sounding angry now. "I'm an officer of the law. Who the hell do you—"

Joanna jammed the pistol against his left eye socket.

"All right, all right," Sherman squeaked. "Chandler was pretty coy about it. I think it's a law firm."

"Name," Joanna said.

"Probably Plymale," Sherman said. "I think that's it. And it's involved with some foundation he's running."

The pistol muzzle was still uncomfortably in Sherman's eye socket. She had released the pressure, but now she restored it.

"I hope you don't want me to believe that old man is just after the diamonds," she said.

Sherman's head was pressed back against the car seat. "No. No," he said. "Somebody else is after the diamonds, but mostly they're after some bones. Want to get the bones for the DNA. For

proof in some lawsuit. Hell of a lot of money involved. And some woman is after the bones, too,
and this Indian here with me, he's supposed to
know where to find them. He was—"

"What's the name of the woman?" Joanna
asked.

"Craig," Sherman said. "Joanna Craig, I
think."

Joanna removed her pistol from Sherman's
face, cocked Sherman's pistol, carefully keeping
her handkerchief over the hammer.

"Anything else you can tell me?"

"That's it," Sherman said. "But I can sure as
hell tell you you're not going to get away with
this. Treating an officer—"

But by then Joanna had thrust Sherman's
heavy pistol through the window, jammed it
against his rib cage, and pulled the trigger.

14

Bradford Chandler had done all the things he needed to do at the South Rim entrance to the Grand Canyon. He'd checked into a very comfortable suite in the Grand Hotel, made a just-in-case visit to the Grand Canyon airport to check on the availability of charter fliers, reserved a jeep for a guided tour, filled out all the required U.S. Park Service paperwork for touring down into the depths, and collected a little information about the do's and don'ts of canyon tripping. One of the do's was a reminder that this was the "monsoon season" in the mountain west, a season of thunderstorms, and that these tended to produce quick, brief, and dangerous flash floods sweeping down the subsidiary canyons leading down to the Colorado River.

As was his custom, he had picked the most

attractive young female Park Service employee there as his source of information, quickly noted from her ID tag that her name was Mela, and turned on his prep-school charm. He was supposed to meet his aunt here, he told this young lady. She was Mrs. Joanna Craig. But, alas, he was late. Could she tell him if Mrs. Craig had already checked in to get the required permits and some advice? The young lady, trained to be helpful to tourists, probably didn't need the encouragement of the Chandler charm. She checked.

Yes, Mela said, a Ms. Joanna Craig had indeed checked in for a visit down into the canyon.

"It was yesterday," she said, returning Chandler's smile. "You're even later than you thought."

"Maybe I can still catch her," he said. "Is she staying at that big hotel?" He dug his notebook from his jacket pocket, flipped through pages long enough to suggest a search. "We're planning to go down the Hopi Salt Shrine Trail. Did she say anything about that? Did she say which trail she would be taking?"

Chandler left with a no to both questions and a warning from the Park Service aide that going down the Salt Trail would require dealing with the Hopi authorities. It was restricted for Hopi religious use and it probably would not be possible for him to go down there. His next stop was the hotel. Yes, a Ms. Joanna Craig was registered. He dialed her room number from the house phone. No answer. No need for his "Sorry, wrong number" excuse. That accomplished, he drove to a tourist parking lot and found himself a place to sit with shade and a view. There he waited for his cell phone to ring and get the word from Sherman that would begin the final phase of this project.

Sherman had called earlier, reporting success. He had located the home of Tuve's mother, found Tuve there, identified himself as a deputy sheriff sent to take Tuve back to Gallup to clear up some problem about bonding him out. Then Sherman said he'd told Tuve that he didn't believe he'd killed the man at the Zuni shop, that he wanted to help Tuve find the old man who had swapped him the diamond and thereby prove his innocence.

"Cut it short," Chandler had said. "Where is he now?"

"Out taking a leak," Sherman said. "We can talk?"

"Well, make it quick. Where do we meet?"

Sherman had said he didn't know yet. "He

says he has to go down something they call the Salt Trail to get close to the place he met this bird, but he says nobody can go down without doing the proper religious things. You need to understand I'm having trouble talking him into it. So far, the best he'll agree to is to show me the place on the rim where the trail starts. He says he'll do the blessing thing with us, give us some pollen and prayer sticks to use to protect us from the spirits, but he won't go down with us."

"The hell he won't! What's wrong with you, Sherman? I understood you know how to get reluctant people to do what they don't want to do."

"He says it's not his fault. Says their Guardian Spirits keep people who aren't sup-posed to be there from using that trail." Sherman chuckled. "He says these spirits are sort of like us humans, except they have two hearts, still talk to the animals, have all sorts of powers. And they'll make us fall over the edge, rocks drop on us, snakes biting us, that sort of thing. Says he'll help us but he won't go down with us. Anyway, he's going to guide me to a parking place at the rim now, where the climb down starts, and when I get there, I'll let you know. It can't be very far from the South Rim entrance. You want me to wait for you there? What's the plan?"

"Look, Sherman. It won't do a damn bit of good to climb down there if he's not going down with us. We have to have him there to be our guide."

"I told him that. Then he said it would be easy for us, and he told me exactly how to get from the end of the trail to the place he was sitting when the man showed up with the diamond, and the other directions we'll need."

"Let's hear 'em," Chandler said.

Sherman explained the directions—the number of feet from water's edge, number of paces down the river, number of paces around a corner of the cliff to the mouth of a drainage slough where he thinks the old man lives, number of minutes Tuve said it took the man to return.

"I think we could do it without him," he said.

"Maybe we could," Chandler said, "but there's too much money riding on this for us to settle for maybe."

"I wasn't intending to settle for any maybe, either," Sherman said. "He'll take us down."

Chandler said, "Yeah?" Emphasis on the skeptical sound.

"Come on, Chandler," Sherman said. "You already reminded me I had a rep for getting people to do what they didn't want to do. You need to remember I ran a police department criminal investigation unit. I haven't forgotten the old tricks. I learned what would get cooperation out of all sorts of people. People a lot tougher than this dumb little Indian."

Hearing Sherman say that restored a lot of Chandler's confidence. The man did have a reputation, a bad one in some circles, for his skill at getting reluctant suspects to reveal where bodies had been hidden, the identities of cohorts, and other crucial information—facts that helped the cause of law enforcement far more than the prospects of the persons accused.

"All right, then," Chandler had said. "How about the other stuff on that list I gave you. What did you find out about the woman who bonded Tuve out?"

"She's interesting," Sherman said. "Her name—the one she's using, anyway—is Joanna Craig, from New York, and from what I've been hearing from various people in the law-and-order business, she was out here a couple of times earlier trying to find her father's grave."

Sherman waited a response to that. Got none.

"Probably the woman you told me about," he added.

"Go on," Chandler said.

"Doesn't that surprise you?"

"Not much," Chandler said.

"It surprised me," Sherman said. "It makes me uneasy when I don't know what I'm poking into."

"Well, the man we're working for told me there's a lawsuit involved in this somehow. An old inheritance dispute. Nothing we need to know about. Just tell me more about the woman."

"Well, she said her dad's name was Clarke and he was killed in that collision of the two airlines that killed so many people back in the 1950s. She told people she was looking for where her daddy was buried. Wanted to visit the grave."

"But she didn't find it?"

"Guess not," Sherman said. "I think that collision, and the fires that followed it, left a real mess. Had to gather up body parts in bags. And a lot of them burned."

Remembering Sherman's attitude brightened

Chandler's mood. He relaxed, enjoying the cool shade, enjoying the amazing, incredible view. Like every other adult American, he had seen so many dazzling photographs of this canyon that it had become a cliché. But Chandler was thinking those photographs had never captured what he was seeing now. He was struck by the mind-boggling immensity of this hole worn out of the earth crust, officially 277 miles of it on the guide book map he had bought, from the Glen Canyon Dam to Lake Mead, not just one canyon but hundreds of them, cutting through layers and layers and layers of stone and other minerals, lava flow and ocean-bottom sediment being hurried into the Colorado River and onward toward the Pacific by the inexorable force of gravity and running water. He was thinking suddenly of his terminal year as a college student, just before his macho appetite for sexual adventures got him arrested and then expelled, thinking of the geology class, of old Dr. Delbert projecting color slides of these same cliffs on the screen and trying to lead them upward from the pale yellow strata near the bottom he called Tapeats Sandstone. "Over that," he says, "is Bright Angel Shale. That gray on top of that is Muav Limestone." And upward, through other layers, colors, ages, with Dr.

Delbert jabbing the screen with his pointer, until they finally reached the dark strip of Hermit Shale, and into the Coconino Sandstone and the Toroweap Formation.

And thus it would go, with Delbert's creaky old voice stripping off the layers of the Colorado Plateau from the core of a newly formed planet to the last volcanic age, hardly a millennium past. It was the only class that Chandler had really enjoyed. The only class that had seriously interrupted his preoccupation with the seduction of the daughters of the super-rich. They were always there, all around him, nodding and giggling through these lectures. He thought now he should have become a geologist.

He was considering that when another cloud formation made its way across the canyon, changing the light pattern, reminding him that time was passing, that Sherman still hadn't called. Why not?

Chandler dug his cell phone out of its belt holster and punched in the number Sherman had given him. It rang, and rang, and rang, and rang. He checked the number. It was correct and it was still ringing. Suddenly a voice.

"Yes."

"Sherman?"

No answer. Then: "Who is this calling?"

Odd, Chandler thought, but it sounded like Sherman. Sort of. Had that no-nonsense "cop talking" ring to it.

"It's Chandler, dammit. Who were you expecting? And where the hell are you? We're wasting too much time. Is Tuve cooperating?"

"What is your business with Mr. Sherman?" the voice said. "Identify yourself."

"Just a moment," Chandler said. "Can you hear me all right? I can barely hear you." He rechecked the number he'd punched. It was Sherman's. But he was, almost certainly, talking to a cop. Which meant something had gone very wrong.

"Can you hear me now?" Chandler asked.

"Perfectly," the voice said.

"Well, I'm very curious about this. You seem to have Sherman's phone. Where's Sherman?"

"You were going to tell me who you are. And where you're calling from."

"Oh, yes," Chandler said. "I'm Jim Belshaw. And I'm calling from the Best Western at Flagstaff. Sherman was supposed to come and meet me here. How come you have his telephone?"

"How come you have his number?"

Chandler thought for a moment about how to make his voice sound angry. "Well, you just better ask him that. But let me talk to him. What the hell's going on? He was supposed to be here an hour ago. Is he all right?"

"You a friend?"

"Yes. Yes I am. Has something happened to him?"

"I'm Officer J. D. Moya, Arizona State Police. And Mr. Belshaw, I want you to stay right where you are until I can get someone there to talk to you."

"Sure. I'll be here at the Best Western. Did something happen to him? Can I do something to help?"

"I hate to tell you this," Officer Moya said, "but the man in the car is in critical condition."

"Critical condition?" Chandler said. "Car accident? Or what?"

"Shot," Moya said. "Do you know why he carried a gun?"

That left Chandler speechless. But only for a moment.

"Somebody shot him? Carjacking, was it? Or maybe an accident. But I didn't even know he had a gun."

Moya didn't respond to that. He said, "What

was he doing parked out by the rim of the Grand Canyon?"

"I have no idea," Chandler said. "Was he alone? Have you caught whoever shot him? I'd be surprised if he'd be picking up a hitchhiker. Or does it look like he shot himself?"

"This investigation has just started, Mr. Belshaw. I'm not in a position to release any information."

Chandler considered this for a moment. How long would it take Arizona State Police to discover there was no Jim Belshaw at the Flagstaff Best Western? Probably just a few minutes. Moya would radio the state cop office in Flagstaff, tell them to send someone over. Then what? When the crime scene crew arrived, and a regular criminal investigator got there, they'd be looking at that little notebook Sherman carried. Would they find Brad Chandler's name written in it? Would they find Chandler's cell phone number? An awfully good chance of that. And maybe the Grand Hotel number.

"Officer Moya," Chandler said. "If somebody shot Sherman, I want to see him punished. I probably don't know anything that would help, but if I knew more about what you found, maybe that would trigger a memory. For example, I think he was planning to take a hike down into the canyon. Was there any hiking stuff in his vehicle? For example, he told me once he knew an Indian who he was going to hire as a guide if he went. So if he was doing that, maybe there would be two sets of camping stuff, or hiking stuff, in the car."

This caused a moment of silence on the Moya end of the conversation.

"Well, thank you for the offer, Mr. Belshaw. But you were wrong about that. I saw what seemed to be just one backpack in the car. But then we don't mess around with the scene of a violent crime like this until the crime scene crew gets here with all its stuff. I just reached in to get a look at his billfold for an identification, and noticed the blood and that big pistol down on the floor. That's about all. Hold on just a minute."

Chandler held on, nervously, hearing the sounds of Moya using his radio.

"Mr. Belshaw, you sure you gave me that Flagstaff hotel right? We radioed in. Our Flagstaff office said Best Western doesn't have any Belshaw registered."

Chandler managed a laugh. "That's because I just pulled into the front entrance here, decided to call Sherman before I checked in, and got all this bad news. I'll go in now and see if they're still holding my reservation. I'll check in and wait. But with Sherman in bad shape, I may not want to stay here in Flagstaff."

"Hey," Moya said. "Stay there. We need to talk to you."

"We're breaking up on this damn cell phone now," Chandler said. "I can't hear you. Just static. Can you read me? Hello? Hello? Officer Moya. Hello? Well, if you can still hear me, I'll check in here. I want to find out what happened to Sherman."

With that, Chandler just listened. Heard Moya yelling at him. Heard Moya cursing. Finally heard Moya give up and break the connection. Then he shut off his own cell phone, shook his head, and started working on the problems this had left him.

The worst one was that notebook Sherman carried in his jacket pocket. There might be some chance Sherman hadn't jotted his name in his book. An awfully good chance he'd noted his telephone number at the Grand Hotel. It wouldn't take much detective work to send them after the man who had called Sherman's cell phone number. But there was nothing he could do about that now.

What he had to do now was find out what happened to Billy Tuve. Had Tuve shot Sherman? Maybe, but it didn't seem likely. If not, who had? Probably one of those other people Plymale had warned him were trying to find the diamonds. Or, as Plymale wanted him to believe, to find the bones. And his job for Plymale was just to keep that from happening. He could probably have accomplished that simply and easily by erasing Tuve from the game. But he had never trusted Plymale. Killing Tuve would have wiped out his chance for his big payoff—a satchel full of prime diamonds.

And now where was Billy Tuve? The competitive team Plymale had described seemed to have eliminated Sherman. From what little he had learned from that damned Arizona state cop, Tuve's stuff hadn't been left behind in Sherman's car. From that, Chandler's logical mind developed the only logical conclusion. The bad guys had come for Tuve. Sherman had resisted. They shot Sherman. They took Tuve away with them, and the only possible use they had for him was identical to Chandler's own. They'd take him to the canyon bottom and use him to find the diamonds. But where? Somewhere very close to the termination of the Hopi Salt Trail, near where the Hopis harvested their ceremonial salt. The jeep-driver guide he had hired to take him to the bottom tomorrow had been full of information about sacred places in the canyon, and the Salt Shrine was near the point where the Little Colorado Canyon dumped its water into the Colorado River. No jeep trail would take them anywhere near that, the driver said, but he could drop them at the head of a trail he'd noticed in his **Hiking the Grand Canyon** book that ended at the river, just an easy walk upstream to the shrine.

Back at his car, Chandler opened the trunk and took out a small aluminum valise. He unlocked it on the front seat and extracted two cans—one a Burma Shave shaving cream dispenser, the other a can of Always Fresh deodorant, both of which had been reengineered by some previous owner so that their tops screwed off, and both of which had been slipped out of an old evidence locker. Chandler presumed they'd previously been used to carry purchase-size packs of crack cocaine. He imagined them tucked in a grocery store sack with bread, soup cans, etc., offering a relatively safe way for the dope dealer to smuggle the stuff to the user. For him, they offered a simple way to get his pet little .25-caliber pistol past airport security x-ray machines.

Now he screwed off the tops, extracted pistol barrel, working parts, magazine, etc., wiped off the thick deposit of shaving cream covering the parts, blew the cream out of the barrel, cleaned it with a rod he kept in the can for that purpose, and reassembled the weapon. He'd had it made at a specialty machine shop in Switzerland on one of his skiing trips there, and it worked with typical Swiss efficiency. He clicked a round into the chamber, ejected it into his hand, and put it back into the chamber.

It worked perfectly. When Ms. Joanna Craig arrived with Tuve at the Hopi shrine tomorrow, he'd be down there waiting.

15

Joe Leaphorn found he had a way to get in touch with Sergeant Chee after all. He found Chee's cell phone number where he had jotted it on the margin of his desk calendar. And now that cell phone began ringing in Chee's jacket pocket. Chee was standing at the rim of the Grand Canyon, watching Cowboy Dashee planting some painted prayer sticks at an odd-looking rock formation.

Chee snorted out a Navajo version of an expletive, extracted the phone, clicked it on, and said, "Chee."

"Joe Leaphorn," Leaphorn said. "Are you still interested in that Billy Tuve business?"

"Sure," Chee said.

"I mean, trying to find where he got that

diamond? If you are, I've heard some things that might be useful."

"Still very interested," Chee said. "Not that any of us have much hope of finding anything."

That produced a silence. "But I'll bet you're going anyway, though. Right?"

Chee glanced around him. Cowboy was standing beside his car, helping Bernie with something. "Lieutenant," he said. "This Billy Tuve is Cowboy's cousin. Brain-damaged guy. And Cowboy has always been there for me when I needed a hand. From way back in high-school days. I think Cowboy's going to climb down and make this search even if there isn't any real hope. We're sort of trying to decide that now."

"You said 'any of us.' You and Cowboy and Tuve?"

"Cowboy and me and Bernie Manuelito. Tuve was supposed to come, but when Cowboy went to get him, he was gone. Somebody showed up at his mother's house and he went off with them. That makes finding anything even more doubtful."

"Probably the sheriff's office came and got him. Sounds like the bond deal went sour. Why is Bernie going?"

"It wasn't the sheriff's office," Chee said. "Maybe it was the woman who bailed him out."

"Odd," Leaphorn said. "But why is Bernie going? That's a hell of a tough climb."

"I don't know why she's going."

Leaphorn laughed. "Want me to make a guess?"

"Why don't you just go ahead and tell me what you called for," Chee said, sounding unhappy. Bernie was standing beside him now, holding a backpack, asking **Who?** with a hand gesture.

Chee let her wait while Leaphorn related what Louisa had told him about the reward for the arm bones, about the rumors growing out of the airline disaster she'd been hearing among the canyon-bottom tribes. "You think any of that will help?"

Chee sighed. "Enough to tip the scales, maybe. Sounds like that hander-out-of-diamonds might still be alive, anyway."

"Who is it?" Bernie asked. "Is that Billy Tuve?"

"Lieutenant Leaphorn," Chee said, "Bernie is here now. Why don't you ask her why she wants to climb down there?" And he handed Bernie the cell phone.

"Lieutenant," Bernie said, grinning at Chee, "it's just like I told Jim. I think it would be fun. And he and Cowboy need somebody to look after them."

"Be careful," Leaphorn said.

"I will," Bernie said. "You know where I live. I'm good at climbing up and down rocks."

"I didn't mean just that, Bernie," Leaphorn said. "I guess you know that the FBI has been pulled into this. Got Captain Pinto to work on it. The federals wanted him to find out everything possible about a diamond that Shorty McGinnis was supposed to have. That means Washington got interested in it, and that means it's a big deal for somebody or other."

"Sergeant Chee told me a little about it," Bernie said.

"He probably doesn't know much more than I do," Leaphorn said. "I hope he told you he and Cowboy weren't the only ones after those diamonds."

"I don't think he did," Bernie said.

"Plus, there's an offer of big money for the bones of one of the victims. For burial."

"Is there more to it than just that?"

"Who knows for sure? But anyway, young lady, remember if Washington is involved, it means very influential people are interested, and that usually means a lot of money is in the balance. That can make it dangerous. So be careful. And try to keep in touch. Just in case you need some help keeping them out of trouble, let me know when you get down to the river if there's a way to call from there."

Getting down to the river took almost six hours, which Dashee thought wasn't too bad, even though he had done it in his late teens in something under five. He'd taken a little extra care at the points where the faithful left little pollen offerings to the Salt Trail's protective spirits and choked off his habit of exchanging barbs with Chee.

Dashee's uneasy silence was not just nervousness caused by worry about what the reaction might be among the spirits that oversaw Hopi behavior. He was also worried about the reaction of the elders in his own clan and kiva if they learned he had escorted two Navajos down this sacred pathway. To strictly traditional Hopis, the Dinee were still remembered as "head breakers"—barbarians so uncivil that they slew enemies with the old "rock on the skull" technique.

For Bernie, standing on the sand catching

her breath, this descent was already a sort of dream, part of a thrilling close-up look at the nature she loved at its rawest beauty. And it had been a nerve-racking experience as well, where a wrong step on a loose stone could have sent her plunging down five hundred feet, to bounce off a ledge, and fall again, and bounce again, until the journey terminated with her as a pile of broken bones beside the Colorado River.

On the way down, to believe what she was seeing, Bernie found herself recalling the reading she'd done to prepare herself for this. That wavering streak of almost-white between the salmon-colored cliffs catching the sun would be Mesozoic era sandstone, reminders of sand dunes buried when the planet was young, and the bloody red in the strata above that would be staining from dissolved iron ore, and the name for that, required on Professor Elrod's geology exam, was hematite, and that thought would be jarred away by an inadvertent downward glance which showed her death. Death just as many seconds away as were required for her to fall, and fall, and fall, until the body of Bernadette Manuelito, more formally known for Navajo ceremonial purposes as Girl Who Laughs, smashed into the riverbank below and became nothing more than a bunch of broken, loosely connected body parts.

Now this journey into her imagination was interrupted by Cowboy Dashee.

"Bernie, what's your idea about that?"

"About what?"

"About what we've been talking about," Dashee said, sounding slightly impatient. "Here we are, right where we were going, and Billy's not here. So what's next? How do we start conducting this search?"

Having no useful idea, Bernie shrugged. "Maybe Billy got here before we did and got tired of waiting for us. How about looking around for him?"

Bernie was looking around herself when she said that, seeing a vast wilderness of cliffs in almost every direction, hearing the roar of water tearing over the rapids and above the thunder of the river, the chorus of whistles, trills, and bong sounds that must have been caused by the various species of frogs that inhabited the canyon. Combined, it made her suggestion sound silly.

"Well, at least we could try," she added.

"I guess that's about all we can do now," Chee said. "Somebody should wait here, where they could see him if he's still coming down the trail, or if he's already down, meet him if he comes back looking for us."

He looked at Dashee. Dashee nodded. He looked at Bernie. "Bernie, you wait here. If Tuve shows up, keep him here until Cowboy and I get back."

"Sergeant Chee," Bernie said, loud enough to be heard over the roar of the river and the clamor of the mating-season frogs, and maybe even a little louder than that, "I want to remind you that I am no longer Officer B. Manuelito of your Navajo Tribal Police squad. I am a private regular citizen."

"Sorry," Chee said, sounding suitably repentant. "I just thought—"

"Okay. I'll stay here," Bernie said. Dashee was grinning at her.

"Thanks," Chee said. "I'm going to suggest that I work my way downstream looking for that sort of side canyon Tuve mentioned, and get back here in . . . let's say ninety minutes or so. Quicker if we've found something. And Cowboy, would you do the same upstream? Up to the confluence where the Little Colorado runs in to the big river and—"

"Got it," Dashee said.

Bernie leaned her weary self against a convenient boulder, let her body slip slowly down it until she was sitting comfortably on a sandstone slab. She watched Cowboy working his way along the cluster of boulders upstream until he disappeared behind the curve of the cliff. She watched Chee moving downstream along the very edge of water, keeping his eyes on the ground. She found herself wishing he would look back, at least a glance, but he didn't. Found herself wishing she hadn't sounded so grouchy. Hadn't **been** so grouchy. When he got back, she would tell him she was sorry. Tell him she was tired. Which was true. And now she would just wait. Maybe find one of those noisy frogs. Tree frogs probably, or maybe red-spotted toads. Take a look at the algae on those damp rocks at water's edge. Think her thoughts. Wish it hadn't taken Jim Chee so long to realize that he had fallen in love with her. Wish she had recognized his hang-ups and made her interest in him a little more obvious. Even a **lot** more obvious.

And after a lot of that, the shadows would be working up the canyon walls, and Jim and Cowboy would be back, and they would make a little fire, probably, and eat some of the stuff they had brought, and talk a lot and roll out their sleeping bags, and Jim would probably want to put theirs close together and a distance from Dashee's, and she would have to deal with that. Her clan taught its daughters that too much intimacy before nuptial promises were officially and ceremonially confirmed before both clans and both families tended to have very bad effects in the married years to come. Therefore, as her mother had put it, "some sand should be kept between you and your police sergeant" until that had happened.

So she would sit here and watch the changing light change the colors on the cliffs, and wait, and think about how good it would be when all this indecision was behind her. But that sort of happy thinking kept drifting away into questions. Was Jim really the man she thought he was, that he seemed to be? Or was he the hard-voiced sergeant who would never, ever really be her man? Was what she was doing at this very moment— following his orders, waiting for the next instructions, waiting to be told what was going on—indicative of what she was getting into? She didn't think so. In fact, she didn't even want to think about it. She wanted to think about where she was—at the very middle of the stupefying grandeur of this canyon, surrounded by all its weird variations of the natural world she knew from the Earth Surface World a mile above her head.

About then the changing light must have touched off some sort of signal to the biology about her. Suddenly the violet-green swallows were out, doing their acrobatic dives, skimming the water for rising insects. Somewhere behind her an owl was out early, making some sort of call that only her oldest uncle could translate, and the spotted toads were adding their grunts to the general birdsong symphony.

Why was she just sitting here? Bernie asked herself. She zipped open the top of her backpack, got out her water bottle, hung her birdwatcher binoculars over her shoulder, then dipped back into the pack for her birder's notebook. She tore out a blank back page, took out her pen, and started writing.

MR. TUVE—I AM WALKING UP RIVER A WAY. BACK SOON. WAIT HERE FOR US.
Bernie

She left the note on the boulder where she had been sitting, put another rock at a corner to hold it down, and started walking—first over to the cliff-side tamarisk trees to investigate a bird nest she'd noticed there, and then down toward an outcropping that a long time ago (probably a few billion years ago) had formed a lava flow obstruction and a noisy little rapid in the Colorado.

The flotsam kicked out at the rapid revealed nothing she hadn't expected, being mostly debris washed down one or another of the little streams that flowed in from the cooler, wetter mesa tops a mile above. She identified the hulls of piñon nuts, Ponderosa needles, twigs from Utah junipers, and a variety of grass samples, many probably blown in but some local needle grass which thrived in this hot, dry bottom. Nothing here she hadn't expected.

Through her binoculars, she checked the place where Jim and Dashee had left her. No sign of them or of Tuve, nor did she spot anyone on the few points high up in the cliffs of the Salt Trail where she thought he might be descending. She focused in as sharply as she could on the boulder where she had left her note. She couldn't see that, either. That either meant that one of the men had come back, found it, and was now (she hoped) awaiting her, or that Tuve had arrived, taken it, and went on his way. Or it meant that these lenses were just not potent enough for her to make it out from where she was standing.

She focused down the cliffs. The angle of the sunlight now made it clear why one of the early explorers she had read—John Wesley Powell, she thought it was—had described them as "parapets." They formed a seemingly infinite row of light and shadow, sort of like looking down a picket fence, with each shadowed space representing a place where drainage from the mesa top had—down through a million or so years of draining off snowmelt and rainwater—eroded its own little canyon in its race to get to the Colorado and on to the Pacific Ocean.

Those canyons would be more interesting than the scene at the riverside. And a side canyon was what both Jim and Cowboy were looking for. An undercut place where their fantastical dispenser of diamonds was living, or had been living. Presuming he had ever existed, which had always seemed doubtful to Bernie.

She skirted past the rapids outcrop and walked downstream. The first opening in the cliff was a dead end for her purposes, blocked with brush and a jumble of boulders swept down by some long-past flash flood. She pushed her way through the barrier far enough to see it offered not much possibility of a cave large enough for occupation.

More walking, with brief checks into four other drain-off cuts in the cliffs, brought her to a more promising-looking drainage mouth. She had been noticing now and then the tracks left by Jim's boots, mostly in the damp sand very close to the putty-toned water of the Colorado. Now she saw them again. They led across the blow sand leading into the mouth of the same opening that attracted her. They went in, out again, then back toward the river, and on downstream.

Ah, well, Bernie thought, he'd be coming back after a while, and when the shadows were longer, the temperature would drop. Her schoolgirl trip into the canyon had been made in the cooler days of late autumn. She'd read that summer heat at the canyon bottom sometimes soared as much as twenty degrees above the temperature on the mesa a mile above. Now she believed it. Even in the shade, it seemed dangerously torrid. She walked up the slot far enough to find a spot where the interior cliffs hadn't been cooking all day under the Southwestern sun. She'd rest awhile and cool off.

Typical of Bernadette Manuelito, the rest period was brief. She noticed tracks of Chee's boots again, scuffing across the thin layer of blow sand near the opposite wall. She'd test the tracking skills she'd been taught in her tour with the Border Patrol.

The tracks disappeared in a tangle of dead, dry tumbleweeds and assorted other sticks and stems, then showed up again where the most recent runoff had left the stone floor bare and subject to scuffing marks. It was, of course, a strictly up-slope walk, and it soon came to a junction where a smaller post-rainstorm stream joined the major flow. She was able to find Chee's tracks only a few yards up the narrower canyon, and then they resumed their climb up the bigger one and came to another junction, this one through a very narrow cut in the cliffs, at which point there was another very short side trip of boot marks.

From this, a comparatively cool downdraft flowed, bringing with it the aroma of the high-country flora—piñon resin, cliffrose, and the slightly acid smell of claretcup cactus. It was comfortable and pleasant here. The bedrock under her feet was damp with a minuscule trickle of water from a narrow horizontal seepage between layers of stone on the opposite wall. A swarm of midges was dining on a growth of moss there, and below them squatted one of the spotted toads common to the deep canyon. He sat so utterly motionless that Bernie wondered for a moment if he was alive. He answered that question with a sudden leap, and scuttled across the stony floor.

Why? Bernie quickly saw the answer. The head of a small snake emerged from under a fallen slab, slithered onto the bedrock floor after the toad. It stopped. Coiled. Swiveled its head and its tongue emerged, testing the air for the strange odor of Bernie, a new species of intruder in the snake's hunting ground.

Bernie had been conditioned from toddling years to look upon everything alive as fellow citizens of a tough and unforgiving natural cosmos. Each and all, be they schoolgirl, scorpion, bobcat, or vulture, had a role to play and was endowed with the good sense to survive—provided good sense was used. Thus Bernie was not afraid of snakes. Even rattlesnakes, which this one obviously was, because after coiling he had raised his terminal tip and sent his species' nameplate warning signal.

But this one was pink, which brought a huge smile to Bernie's face and the immediate thought of Dr. William Degenhardt, her favorite professor at the University of New Mexico. Degenhardt, an internationally acclaimed herpetologist, was an authority on snakes, salamanders, and other such cold-blooded beasts, and was known, in fact, as their friend, with a huge portrait of a coiled rattler on his living room wall. Bernie remembered his lectures fondly, and in one the Pink Grand Canyon Rattlesnake was the subject—not just because it was rare but because it was such a wonderful demonstration of how a species could adapt itself in size, color, and hunting techniques to the weird environment the Grand Canyon offered.

Bernie found herself wishing she had a camera. She could hardly wait to tell Degenhardt about this. Maybe she could catch the thing and take it back to him. But the professor would never approve of such a disruption of nature. Besides, she couldn't keep it alive in her backpack. So she simply stared at it, shifting her memory into the Save mode, and recorded every variation in color, shade, and tone, size and number of rattles, shape of head, and so forth—all of the features the professor would want to compare with the illustrations in his textbook on such beasts. But the snake tired eventually of this scrutiny, thrust out his tongue to test the air a final time, and slithered away to hide himself again back under a stone slab.

The cry of a peregrine falcon snapped Bernie out of thinking about snakes and professors, and back into the duty to which Sergeant Chee had assigned her. It was time to climb out of this slot and find a place from which she could see if Tuve had climbed down the Salt Trail to join this expedition. Or if Chee, or Dashee, or both were awaiting her down at the Salt Woman Shrine.

Reaching the spot that looked most promising as a lookout post involved scrambling up a broken section of the opposing wall of the canyon she had followed up from the river. It was a tough climb, made even slower because the Pink Rattler had reminded Bernie that snakes like hanging out in hidden little spaces under rocks. She was very, very careful where she put her hands while pulling herself up to the shelf she had chosen.

It was a good choice. From that vantage point, her binoculars could scan down into a substantial stretch of the Colorado River, and two small waterfalls flowing out of cliff-side drainage across the river. Upriver her view took in the stream flowing in from the Little Colorado, forming the deep, cool pool of bluish water near the Salt Woman Shrine and lightening the muddy tone of the Colorado.

More important, she could see the spot where Sergeant Chee had commanded her to await his return. Well, the sergeant hadn't returned from his hunt downriver. Nor did Cowboy Dashee seem to be back from his excursion up the river. No sign of Tuve, either. Unless he had come and gone again. For that matter, maybe Chee and Dashee had been back and were off again hunting for her.

Bernie felt a touch of uneasy guilt. Jim really hadn't asked much of her. Just to help out a little on their mission of mercy for Billy Tuve. She could have postponed her botanical research project. Jim's opinion of her would be dented some if he returned and found her missing.

But that twinge of guilt was quickly submerged under another thought. Unlikely as it seemed, maybe they had actually found what they were looking for—the haunt of this fellow who had, so they believed, dished out diamonds to passersby. Perhaps they had reached their goal and just hadn't bothered to come and invite her to join in the excitement of the discovery. Or maybe Chee had broken a leg climbing the rocks. Or Dashee had been hurt and Chee had gone to help him. Or maybe they were just looking longer, and being slower, than she had expected.

Bernie had found her bird-watching binoculars in a military surplus store in Albuquerque, and they had been designed for a more serious purpose, being much more optically powerful than normal bird-watchers need, and much heavier than anything they would want to lug around on their walks. She lowered them. Wiped the perspiration from her eyebrows, relaxed her wrists for a moment, and then raised them again for another look.

A man walked right into her circle of view. He took a water bottle out of the pocket on the side of his trouser leg, pushed off his hat, and took a drink. The man was big and blond and looked young. He was also barefoot. Bernie watched him walk gingerly through the hot sand to the boulder where she had rested. He sat on it, reached into the shade behind it, and extracted a pair of hiking boots. He pulled the socks out of the boots, massaged each foot carefully, and then reshod himself.

Who could he be? Probably just another tourist. But maybe not. River runners boating down the Colorado were not allowed to drop people off here, out of deference to the Hopi religious sites. He could have walked down, of course. He was still massaging his feet and that suggested that he might have. But the Salt Trail was the only fairly easy access and it, too, was forbidden to him without Hopi permission and an escort.

Bernie left him caring for his feet and re-scanned the scene around her. Still no sign of Jim, Cowboy, Billy Tuve, or anyone else. The only sign of life she detected was a herd of four horses taking their leisure under the shade of what seemed to be Russian olive trees across the river. She switched her binoculars back to the blond man. He had his hat on now and a pair of binoculars—even larger than hers—to his eyes. He seemed to be slowly and methodically scanning the slopes around him. Back and forth, up and down, looking for something. For what?

Bernie had a sudden and alarming thought that he might be looking for her. That he might have already spotted her. That he might be someone who had seen one of those posters Chee and Dashee had talked about, offering the reward for recovering the bones. That he might be somebody involved in whatever had caused Washington to nudge the FBI into this. That he might be dangerous.

Bernie got up, took another look at the place where Chee had abandoned her near the Salt Woman Shrine. Cautious now, barely peeking over the edge of the stone shelf.

The big blond man had his back turned toward her now, looking the other way, apparently studying the higher reaches of the Salt Trail. Waiting for Tuve, she guessed. And that thought reminded her of **Waiting for Godot**, and the time they had wasted in her Literature 411 class discussing whether Godot would ever arrive, and what difference it would make if he did. And now wasn't she sort of a perfect match for Beckett's ridiculous characters?

To hell with it. She would find Chee and tell him she was going home. Or wherever she could get from here. Or maybe just turn this into a sort of botanical field trip and let the sergeant and the deputy sheriff chase their mythological diamond dispenser on their own.

Climbing down the rock slide from her high perch was easier than ascending it, but trickier. And when she reached the bottom, she found a woman standing there, watching her and waiting.

16

"Girl," the woman said, "you shouldn't be here. Here it is dangerous for you."

Which left Bernie wordless for a moment. She mumbled the Navajo "Ye eeh teh" greeting, produced a sort of hesitant smile, dusted off her jeans, examined the hand she had scraped on the climb down, and glanced up. The woman was small and elderly, with a dark, weatherworn face and long white hair. She wore a long skirt of much-bleached denim, a long blue shirt, and carried a canvas bag on a strap over her shoulder. A Hopi, maybe, or one of the Supai from across the river, or perhaps from another of the Pueblo people.

Bernie held out her hand. "I am Bernadette Manuelito," she said. "But why is it dangerous?"

"People who don't know Hopi talk, they

call me Mary," the woman said. "But you are a
Navajo, I think. Not just a tourist. I saw you
near the Salt Woman Shrine by the blue pool.
That is a place for the Hopi holy people. Not
for . . . Not for people not initiated into a kiva."

Bernie was embarrassed. "But I came there
with a Hopi. A Hopi who belongs to one of the
kivas that come down the trail to collect salt and
colored clay for its ceremonials. He said it was all
right."

The woman considered that, her expression
stern, but her eyes were on Bernie's injured
hand.

"It bleeds," she said. "Where did you cut it?"

"I slipped climbing down," Bernie said. "I
tried to catch myself. Cut it on a rock."

"I have a salve for that at home," the woman
said. "I sold it where I worked at Peach Springs
and it heals cuts very quickly." She smiled a wry
smile. "Long time ago. I got tired of talking to
tourists all the time."

Bernie opened her backpack and took out
her half-empty water bottle. "You think I should
wash it off?" she asked. "Get the dirt out of it?"

"Is that all the drinking water you have?"

Bernie nodded. "I've been walking a lot. I
guess I should have saved more."

"Up that little canyon there"—the woman pointed—"is a little spring where the water seeps out. It is bitter with what it washes out of the rock. It makes you sick if you drink it. But it would be good for washing that cut."

"I'll do that," Bernie said.

The woman pointed at the bottle. "That's all you have to drink? For how long is that?"

"I'm not sure. Someone is supposed to come and meet me up there near the Salt Woman Shrine. I hope pretty soon."

"Was he a man? He's already there."

Jim had come back! Bernie felt a wave of relief. Followed immediately by apprehension. "A handsome young Navajo policeman? But not wearing his uniform?"

The old woman laughed. "Not any Navajo policeman," she said. "Not unless you have big white-haired Navajo men with blue eyes. But he had a gun like a policeman."

"You saw a gun?"

"A pistol. He was looking at it. Then putting it back under his belt."

"Oh," Bernie said. She looked at the old woman, and the old woman looked at her. Nodded.

"Some sort of trouble?" the woman said.

"Maybe man trouble. That's usually it. So you don't want to go up there right now, is that right? Until the right man comes to meet you."

"Something like that," Bernie said.

The woman smiled. "Then I should give you some more drinking water, daughter. Give you some more time to wait before you dry up. But you should go back down to the big river to wait for your Navajo policeman. Up here it is dangerous."

Bernie nodded.

The woman swung the bag off her shoulder. It was one of those canvas canteens that dry-country cowboys and sheep herders hang from their saddles. She pointed to Bernie's bottle, said, "I will share with you."

"Thank you, Mary," Bernie said. "Do you have enough?"

The woman laughed. "I'm not waiting for a man," she said. "I'm going home. You should be doing that. Not staying so close to where the danger is."

Bernie held out her bottle. Thinking while the woman filled it about the pistol she had seen, and about what she, Bernie, seemed to be getting into here.

"This danger," Bernie said. "Could you tell me what it is?"

Mary considered this. "Have you heard about the Hopi? How we came to be on this Earth Surface World? About our kachinas? Any of that?"

"Some of it," Bernie said. "My mother's father told me something, and my uncle knew something about it. He's a hatalii. A singer."

Mary looked skeptical.

"I guess it was just what they had heard from friends," Bernie said. "Nothing secret."

"You know about Masaw? The one some people call the Skeleton Man?"

"I heard he was the Guardian Spirit of the Hopis on this Earth Surface World."

Mary nodded. "This Glittering World," she said.

"Wasn't he the spirit who greeted the Hopi people when they emerged out of the dark worlds into this one? The one who told you to make migrations to the four directions and then you would find the Center Place of the World? And you should live there? Up on the Hopi Mesas?"

Mary was smiling. "Well," she said. "I guess

that's a version of a little bit of it. The way people in the Bear Clan tell it, anyway. What else
have you heard?"

"I read in the book Frank Waters wrote that
when Masaw met the people emerging from the
underworld, his face was all bloody. That he was
a fearsome-looking kachina. And that he taught
you not to be afraid to die. I think you called him
the Death Kachina."

Mary nodded. "Or sometimes the Skeleton
Man. And some of the old people tell us that in
another way," she said. "In those dark first three
worlds we were forced out because of horrible
crowding. People kept making babies but nobody ever died. We were jammed in together so
tight, they say, that you couldn't spit without
spitting on somebody else. Could hardly move.
People just kept creating more people. Twin
brothers were leaders of the people then. They
found a way to grow a reed through the roof of
the first dark world for us to the second one, and
then, when it got too crowded, on into the third
one, and finally into this one. But still nobody
ever died until Masaw taught people not to be
afraid of death."

Bernie had heard something like this in one
of her anthropology classes, but not this version.

"How did he do that?" she asked.

"One of the clan leaders had a beautiful daughter who was killed by another little girl. Out of jealousy. And that caused trouble between families. So Masaw opened the earth so the clan leader could see his daughter in the world beyond this one. She was laughing, happy, playing, singing her prayers."

"That sounds like the Christian heaven," Bernie said. "Our Navajo beliefs—most of them, anyway—aren't so specific. But you were going to tell me why it's dangerous for me here."

"Because up there . . ." She paused, shook her head, pointed up the canyon. "Up there, they say, is where the Skeleton Man lives. Up there in the biggest canyon that runs into this one. Comes in from the left. They say he painted a symbol on the cliff where it enters. The symbol for the Skeleton Man." Mary knelt, drew in the sand with her finger. The shape she formed meant nothing to Bernie.

"Is the danger because that place is where Masaw, or the Skeleton Man, is living?" Bernie asked, feeling uneasy. "Is that spirit dangerous to people like me?"

Mary shook her head, looking troubled. "Everything gets so mixed up," she said. "The

Supai people have their ideas, and the Paiutes come in here with different ideas, and the priests and the preachers and even the Peyote People tell us things. But I've been hearing that it might be some man, even older than me now. Nobody knew who his parents were. He used to come to Peach Springs and kept telling stories about how Masaw was the one who caused all those bodies to come falling down here into the canyon. Said Masaw made those planes run together. And this man was trying to get people to change their religions around and believe like him. I think he's the one who started calling Masaw the Skeleton Man."

Mary stopped, shook her head, laughed. "When I was just a young woman, he came around to the village and showed us tricks. He had this little deer-skin pollen bag he'd hold up in the sunlight. Like this." She held her right hand high above her head and pinched her thumb and fingers together. "He told us to notice how ugly and brown the pollen pouch looked. That's how this life is, he'd say, but look what you get if you're willing to get rid of this life. To get out of it. And then the pollen sack would turn into this glittering thing sitting on the end of his fingers."

She stared at Bernie, her expression questioning, looking for Bernie's reaction.

"Amazing," Bernie said. She was thinking how the trick might have been done—the thumb and forefinger squeezing the diamond out of the pouch, the pouch disappearing into the palm.

"I saw it myself," Mary said. "That sack just glittered and glittered as he turned it in the sunlight."

"Then what happened?"

"I don't remember exactly. But in a little while, he was holding the pollen pouch again, and it didn't glitter anymore."

"Fascinating," Bernie said.

"My uncle told me he thought it was some sort of trick, but this man said the Skeleton Man gave it to him to prove to people they should be willing to die. The ugly brown pollen pouch was like the life they were living now. After they died, it would be bright and shiny."

"Where did this man come from? Does what he was telling you fit in with what they teach in your kiva?"

"I don't remember as much about the old times as I should," Mary said, looking sad. "I know I was taught them when I was little, but all those years up at Peach Springs talking with all kinds of other people, I forget them. And they got mixed in with other stuff. But I know that even though Masaw looked horrible—they say his face was all covered with blood—he was a friend of the people in some ways."

"Like teaching them not to be afraid to die?"

"Like that," Mary said, smiling. "I remember my mother used to tell that to me. That just two things we know for certain. That we're born and in a little while we die. It's what we do in the time between that matters. That's what the One Who Made Us thinks about when he decides what happens to us next."

Bernie considered that. Nodded. "I think all of us are pretty much alike, whatever our tribe and whatever color we are," she said.

"Everybody also has sense enough to stay away from places that are dangerous," Mary said, staring at Bernie. "Like not poking at a coiled snake with your hand."

Bernie nodded.

"Like not trying to go up where the Skeleton Man lives," Mary added.

"Unless you really need to go. To see if you can save a man who will get locked up in prison if you don't find something there," Bernie said.

Mary took a very deep breath, exhaled it. "So you'll go up that canyon anyway?"

"I have to."

Mary pointed up the canyon. "There's a narrow slot in the cliff wall to your left around that corner. Then on the right, farther up, you'll find another slot, a little wider, and a trickle of water sometimes is flowing out of it. But it's blocked with rocks where part of the cliff fell down, and around those rocks there's the thick brush of the cat's claw bushes. You can't get through that without getting all bloody."

Bernie nodded.

"Girl," Mary said. "You should not go. But be very careful. If you need help, no one would ever find you."

17

Joanna Craig sat on a shelf of some sort of smooth, pale pink stone about two thousand feet above what she guessed must be the Colorado River. It was putty-colored, not the clear blue she had always imagined, and the cliffs across it (and behind her, and everywhere else) soared upward to a dark blue sky, partly crowded with towering clouds—dark on the bottom. Joanna's mood was also at its bottom at the moment, and like the clouds, dark blue.

Joanna was admitting to herself that she had screwed up. She was facing the fact that Billy Tuve, while brain-damaged, had outwitted her. He was gone. She was alone. Worse, due to her own foolishness, she seemed to be walking into a trap. She was leaning forward, elbows on knees, head down, resting everything but her mind, ticking off the mistakes she had been making and looking for solutions.

Maybe the first mistake had been even coming here. But that was no mistake. It was something she had to do. Something, call it her destiny, had caused that damned diamond to appear out of the distant past. Maybe her prayers had caused it. Too many years of praying for a way to get revenge. To see justice done. And finally the diamond had appeared, had been given to a childlike Hopi, had set off a chain of events, led to her lawyer, and had drawn her here, two thousand miles from home, to sit, exhausted, two thousand feet above a dirty river, not knowing what to do.

Of course, she should have kept pressing Tuve about the man who came to talk to him in jail just an hour or two before she had arrived and bonded him out. Who was he? Lawyer, Tuve said. Said his name was Jim Belshaw. Said he would represent Billy, get him out of jail, but Billy had to tell him where he had gotten the diamond. What had he looked like? Big white man, hair almost white, face sort of reddish. Eyes blue. And what had he told this Jim Belshaw about where the diamond had come from? That he didn't know. That this diamond man had just walked a little ways down the river from the blue pool near the Salt Woman Shrine and came back with it. What else? Tuve had just shaken his head. He was finished talking about it. And she had allowed him to get away with that.

Then the narrow little trail bent around a corner of the cliff, and Tuve had pointed downward. Through the binoculars she had seen where the clearer stream from the Little Colorado Canyon poured into the muddy Colorado, and beyond that the blue oblong shape of a pool, which must have been supplied with water by a spring. Down there, she thought, must be the site of the Salt Woman Shrine.

Tuve had been standing behind her. "Ah," he said, and something else. And pointed. She noticed motion. A figure walking along the bank of the pool, disappearing behind the brush trees, reappearing, bending to examine something on the ground. It was a man, apparently, but he was too far below them to tell much else.

"Is that this lawyer?" she had asked. "Is this the Belshaw who came to see you?"

Tuve didn't answer.

"It could be him," Joanna had said. "It's a big man, like you said he was. Right?" She stared through the binoculars, shifted her position as the man moved to where a tamarisk partly shielded him from her view. "Tall," she said. "Looks like he's well dressed for hiking. But with his hat on I can't tell from here if he's blond. Does he look like—"

But Billy Tuve was no longer with her. Not standing behind her on the track. Not anywhere that she could see. Perhaps he had gone back up the trail, around that bend up twenty yards or so. Maybe ducking back into the brush to relieve himself. Joanna stopped thinking and started running.

"Billy!" she shouted. "Mr. Tuve!" But he wasn't at the bend in the trail, or around it. Not as far as she could see. She hadn't realized how tired her legs had become on the long and tricky walk down. She stopped, catching her breath, shaking, trying to see a place up the trail where he might be hiding. There were several. More than she had the energy left to check. But why would he be hiding? Why leave her like this?

Then Joanna had slumped against the cliff wall, sliding down the rough stone, and sitting, back against it, legs drawn up, forehead resting between her knees. The warm, dusty fabric of her jeans reminding her of how thirsty she was. Of how little water was left in her bottle. Trying to fend off despair. Trying to think.

Had Billy Tuve betrayed her? Well, why shouldn't he? He seemed slow and innocent, but he had been smart enough to see she was using him. Yet he had been willing enough to help her—and help her to help him. So why had he abandoned her now? He'd been cooperative, even sympathetic, until he had seen that man down below. Perhaps he had recognized him as the man who had come to the jail. Probably he had. Perhaps he and the blond man had made some sort of deal. Perhaps the man was waiting at the bottom of the trail just to meet Tuve. For Tuve to lead him to the diamonds. This blond would be Plymale's lieutenant. This man she shot was working for him, had called him Bradford Chandler, said he was working for some lawyer named Plymale.

But if Tuve had made a deal with this Chandler, why hadn't he gone on down the trail to meet him? Why had he gone the other way? Was Tuve afraid of the man? If he worked for Plymale, she had a better reason herself to be afraid.

And then she noticed Tuve's canteen.

It was propped neatly on a narrow shelf jutting from the cliff, almost as if she was supposed to notice it. As if Billy Tuve had left it for her to use. She pushed herself up, painfully stiff from the brief rest, and got the canteen. It was heavy and the leather cover was soaked and cool.

She sat again, leaning against the stone, unscrewed the cap, touched liquid with the tip of her tongue. The taste was stale, but it was water. She took a sip, holding it, enjoying it. Modifying the grim and depressing thought that Tuve, whom she had come to like, had abandoned her to die of dehydration with the knowledge that he'd left her enough water to get herself to safety. She had heard that the Hopis, and others, left hidden caches of water containers along some of the trails for emergencies. Tuve would have known where to find such a cache if he needed water. Still, even if this didn't represent a life-endangering sacrifice for him, it was a kind thing to do—curing her despair as well as her thirst.

It also brought her to a decision. She would climb down the Salt Trail to the bottom. She would keep out of sight. Tuve had probably told his jail visitor as much as he'd told her. Maybe he had told him more. If this jail visitor had abandoned his wait for Tuve, perhaps he would begin his hunt for the diamond dispenser on his own. She would follow him wherever it took her.

Joanna rose, dusted off her jeans, poured what was left in her own water bottle into Tuve's canteen, and resumed her descent. Not much hope, really. But she still had her little pistol if it was needed. And what else could she do? The opportunity she had prayed for ever since her mother's death had finally come. A chance to attain justice. And revenge. And maybe, finally, some peace and some happiness. She had to follow where this was leading her. Even if it killed her. As Tuve had told her when they started down the trail, the Hopis had a kachina spirit who once opened a door marked death and showed them a happy life beyond it.

Thinking of that caused her to think of Sherman. Had she killed him? She'd intended to when she pulled the trigger. But maybe he'd lived. Now she found herself hoping he had. Not wanting to have been his executioner.

Joanna produced what might be called a laugh. Whatever lay behind that door, it wouldn't have to be much to be better than the life she'd return to if she didn't complete this search. Whatever was down there in this dreadful canyon, it was her destiny to find it.

18

Bradford Chandler had come to a series of conclusions. The first one was that he was wasting his time waiting for Billy Tuve here at the bottom end of the Hopi Salt Trail. He had found the note signed by someone named "Bernie," which told him that others—at least Bernie and friends—were also expecting Tuve here. That offered interesting implications. Probably they had seen those posters offering the reward. But whatever it meant, he'd wait.

He put the note back exactly where he'd found it, settled into a comfortable place screened by vegetation. He'd stay and see what would happen.

Coming here to meet Tuve had seemed the only choice—despite the outrageous fee the copter pilot had charged to bring him. After all, he could charge that to Plymale, including the fine the pilot would have to pay for violating the National Park Service's no-fly zone. But now he suspected he might be just wasting his time and Plymale's money. He had landed himself in a complicated situation that he didn't understand.

He'd checked around and confirmed that this place met the description Tuve had given him of the trail's terminus—precisely the site where Tuve claimed he'd traded his folding shovel for the diamond. Then Chandler had scanned the cliffs above and upriver, looking for places where he could see portions of the trail's route. His theory was that Tuve would be coming down either in the custody of whoever had shot Sherman or, if Tuve had himself shot Sherman, alone. He'd come because while Tuve was childlike, he was smart enough to know that if he found that cache of diamonds, it would clear him of the robbery/murder charge that confronted him.

From this spot Chandler had located three places where anyone making their way down the trail would be visible through his binoculars. He saw no sign of movement at any of them, lowered the heavy binoculars, rubbed his eyes, and checked around him again. From what Tuve had told him, the diamond dispenser had walked downriver and returned in just a few minutes with the stone he gave to Tuve. Chandler picked up the glasses again and did some scanning downstream.

He saw miles of cliffs, towering clouds now alternating with the dark blue sky in several places. He noticed five or six horses grazing in a small field across the river, more ragged cliffs on his side, and then, abruptly, a flash of light just as his vision moved past it. Chandler swung the binoculars back, saw the flash again, focused in. It came from the top of a relatively low ridge rimmed with brushy dry-country vegetation, with a much higher cliff soaring behind and beyond it.

Amid that vegetation, someone was standing looking at him, or at least looking toward him, through their own set of binoculars. Sunlight reflecting from the lenses must have produced the flashes he'd seen. As much as he could tell at this range, this watcher was wearing a blue shirt and a gray hat. Then the watcher turned, stepped away, and down, and was abruptly out of sight. It was a woman, a small woman. Could it be the Bernie who had left the note?

He stared at the site on the ridge, and the area around it, until his eyes ached, and saw nothing more.

He spent a moment resting his eyes and considering what this must mean. Perhaps a tourist engaged in wandering around? That didn't seem likely in such an unlovely and inhospitable-looking site as that ridge. Why would anyone without a specific interest be making that climb?

Could the woman be Joanna Craig? That ridge seemed to him to be just about where following Tuve's description would take him. And she, too, would have heard the same Tuve story, and perhaps much more. He considered that a moment, then he shifted his gaze to the opposite direction and began another study of the segments of the Salt Trail visible to him above and upriver.

No movement on the highest segment. The second segment was also devoid of any sign of activity. At the lowest level he found what he had hoped to see. He focused on two figures—apparently male and female. An agile one, whom Chandler decided must be Billy Tuve, was leading the way for the fearful and very careful form whom Chandler presumed was none other than Joanna Craig, Plymale's enemy. Ah!

But who, then, was the woman with the binoculars who had been watching him from the ridge down the river? And what was the connection between this Bernie and her friends and Tuve? Chandler considered that question, decided the only answer available to him was through guesswork, and decided it might have something to do with Park Service security. No way of knowing.

He would operate on his original surmise— that Joanna Craig had shot Sherman in his car on the canyon rim at the head of the trail. She had taken custody of Tuve and Tuve was now guiding her on the Salt Trail's winding three thousand-foot plunge toward the Colorado River. Once there, Tuve would lead her to the lair of the diamond dispenser. Her goal was the same as his own. He would simply join the party, help her to use Tuve to lead them both to those diamonds.

Thinking about the possibilities this situation offered caused Chandler to smile—his first of the day.

Forget the diamonds for now. Maybe his first step should be the elimination of Craig from the problem. He would take her identification to prove to Plymale that his task had been accomplished and collect the payment for that. That would simplify things. Then if Tuve actually guided him to the diamonds, he would have them as a bonus.

Chandler sat on what he thought might be the same boulder that Tuve described sitting on when the diamond dispenser had appeared years ago. Better not shoot her, though. Why invite a murder investigation? Better a fatal blow to the head with a rock. Then stuff some rocks in her clothing to weigh her down? Or let her float away? Probably let her float. Make it seem she had fallen, banged her head, landed in the river. How about Tuve? He'd need him to find the diamonds. But why leave a witness? But Bernie and friends were also expecting Tuve. He'd have to wait and see what developed.

Whereupon Bradford Chandler slipped his binoculars back into their case and set about finding the best place to confront Ms. Craig (and Tuve) when she reached the bottom.

And decide exactly what to say to her.

19

Sergeant Jim Chee was standing on the rocky shelf overlooking the up-canyon trail, looking down upon Cowboy Dashee, trying to calculate what Dashee was doing. At first glance Cowboy seemed to be taking off his left boot. But at second glance, Cowboy seemed to have abandoned that project and was attempting to cut off the bottom of his left pant leg with his pocket knife. Chee gave up.

"Cowboy!" he shouted. "What are you doing?"

Dashee dropped the knife and looked up, scowling. "Where the hell have you been?" he said. "You gone deaf, or what? I was hollering until I just about lost my voice."

"You're hurt," Chee said, and began scrambling down the slope. "I've been looking for you. What happened?"

Dashee leaned back, released a huge sigh of relief. "Glad you finally found me," he said. He shook his head. "I slipped. Tried to stop the fall. Left foot caught. Did something to my ankle."

Chee was squatting beside him now, inspecting the offending foot.

"Sprained it?"

"I hope that's it," Dashee said.

"Broke, you think?"

"I guess," Dashee said. "It feels like it. Or maybe it pulled the tendon loose. I was trying to get the boot off before it got too swollen."

Chee rescued Dashee's pocket knife. Gently as possible he cut the remaining strings, eased the boot off, and inspected the ankle.

"Already swollen," he said. "When did it happen?"

"About an hour ago, I guess," he said through gritted teeth. "I was checking on a little side canyon up there."

"How far?" Chee asked.

Dashee managed a strained-sounding laugh. "What difference does that make? But I'd say about an hour's downhill crawl, with a few stops to feel sorry for myself and yell for help."

"Tell you what," Chee said. "I'll carry you down to that deep little pool by the Salt Shrine. That water's cold. You can soak it, and I'll see what I can do about finding some help."

They discussed that suggestion, with Dashee expressing his doubts that Chee could carry him down the narrow and obstacle-rich trail without dropping him (or more likely, both of them) on the ragged boulders. He pressed for an alternate solution in which Dashee's already-slit pants leg would be converted into bandage material, the ankle would be securely bound, and the trip would be made with Dashee hopping along on his good leg and Chee supporting his damaged side.

While the proposed bandaging was being done, they delivered their reports. Dashee had checked out two promising-looking connecting gulches, finding tracks and some interesting petroglyphs from Anasazi days, and was giving up on the second of these when he took his fall. Chee reported that he had taken looks at some undercuts which might have been cave sites—one with some signs it had been lived in long ago. He had made an extensive exploration of a fairly major drainage canyon, finding old tracks, both horse and human, but nothing very promising to suggest it was the home of the diamond dispenser. Then he returned to the place they had left Bernie to await Billy Tuve.

"What did she have to say?"

"She wasn't there," Chee said.

Dashee quit grimacing long enough to look surprised. And then alarmed. "She wasn't? What happened?"

"She left a note on that big flat rock there. She told Tuve she was going to walk up the river awhile, and if he showed up before she got back, then wait for her. And if we showed up, the same for us. Our turn to wait."

Dashee managed a grin. "Sounds like Bernie," he said.

"Yeah," Chee said, looking less happy about it. "Anyway, I waited awhile. Looked around. Found some other tracks there, too. Made by new men's hiking boots. About size eleven or twelve, I'd say. But no sign of anyone there. Then I thought maybe you'd found the diamond man's cave and come back to get her and she'd left with you for a look at it. So I headed up this way and heard you hollering."

Dashee considered that, didn't like the sound of it.

"Hey," he said. "I wonder what happened to her."

"I thought she'd be here with you. Now I'm getting a little worried."

"Maybe another broken ankle," Dashee said. "Hope it's nothing worse. Hope she wasn't hauled away by the size-twelve hiking boots."

"I checked on that. They seemed to be a lot fresher than her tracks. And when her tracks went upriver, they didn't follow."

"Still, it makes you uneasy," Dashee said.

"Let's get you down to the river," Chee said. "I think we can get a call out from there for the National Park rescue people to come and get you. I want to go find her."

20

Successful skip tracers develop through endless practice the craft of concealment. One does not capture the wanted man nor repossess the overdue auto if the culprit sees you first. Almost anywhere in its meandering official 277 miles, the Grand Canyon offers a fine assortment of hiding places. The bottom end of the Hopi Salt Trail was no exception. Bradford Chandler selected a niche in the nearby cliff. It offered shade, a comfortable place to sit, the cover of a growth of tamarisk bushes, and a good view of the final hundred yards of the trail down which Joanna Craig would be coming. While he sat there waiting, he developed and refined his tactics for dealing with the woman.

Since she probably had shot Sherman, she probably had a pistol, and seemed to have no hesitation about shooting it. If she was carrying it in her hand, which he thought unlikely, he would simply shoot her. Why take the risk? More likely it would be tucked away. Perhaps even disposed of, since she would logically expect the police to be looking for her. Anyway, if the pistol was not displayed, he would assume the role of a business-man proposing a deal, which should, if his lies were well told, seem persuasive.

He stretched his legs, took another drink from his water bottle, and went over it again. He'd hardly started that when she appeared, alone, trudging wearily down the final rough segment of the trail, looking dusty, disheveled, and exhausted.

He stood. She stopped at the trail end, stud-ied the area for a minute, then walked past him, not more than a dozen yards beyond the bush he was behind. Then Chandler stepped out behind her.

"Ms. Craig," he said, in a voice just loud enough for her to hear. "I'd like to introduce my-self and talk to you for a few minutes."

Joanna Craig issued a sort of semi-shriek and spun around staring at Chandler, face white, eyes wide, looking terrified.

"Oh," she said. "Oh. Who—" She took a deep breath. "You startled me."

"I'm sorry," Chandler said. "I beg your pardon. You look tired. And it's so hot down here. You should sit down for a moment. Get a little rest. Could I offer you a drink of water?"

"But who are you? How did you know my—" She cut off that question, which told Chandler that she might already know the answer.

"I'm Jim Belshaw," he said. "A sort of private investigator by trade. And I think we have something in common. I'd like to explain myself to you and see if we can work out some sort of partnership."

"Oh," Joanna said. She wiped her hand across her forehead. Studied him.

Chandler pulled back a limb of the bush and pointed to the shady shelf where he'd been sitting.

"No cushions. But it's comfortable." He extracted his water bottle from its pocket and handed it to her. "It's warm and I'm afraid I can't offer you a glass."

Joanna held up a hand, rejecting it, studying him. "What are you doing down here? And . . . and . . . who did you say you were?"

"I'm Jim Belshaw. I work for Corporate Investigations in Los Angeles." He smiled at her, then chuckled. Awaited a response, and added,

"But here in the Grand Canyon today, I'm on my own time. And I'll bet you can guess what I'm doing here."

"Well," Joanna said. She sat on the shelf, closed her eyes, and sighed. "Why don't you just tell me."

"Actually, I was here waiting for a Hopi named Billy Tuve to show up. I watched the two of you coming down the Salt Trail, or whatever they call it. Now you're here but I'm still waiting for Tuve. Is he coming along?"

"Why? What do you want?"

"Why? Because I am looking for a bunch of diamonds," Chandler said. "I think you are, too."

Joanna took a moment to respond to that. The only reason this big, athletic-looking man would know her name, would know about the diamonds connected with it, would be that he was working for Plymale. And if he was working for Plymale, there was a good chance he could accomplish the job the lawyer must have given him by killing her. He was big enough to do it barehanded. And her little pistol was tucked away in her backpack. She looked up at him, trying to read something in the face smiling down at her.

"What makes you think that I'm looking for diamonds?"

"Because they used to belong to your father," Chandler said.

"Oh," Joanna said. No doubt now he was working for Plymale, but then why were they having this conversation? She rubbed her hands down her legs, so tired the muscles were cramping. She looked up again, saw this big young man still staring down at her, awaiting an answer. Let him wait. She needed time to think about this.

"And also because if justice was done, they would be your diamonds now."

He waited again.

"That's correct, isn't it?"

"I think it is," Joanna said. "And I also think you're working for the man who cheated my mother. Took everything away from her. How else could you know all this about me? About my business?"

"I don't know it for sure. It's what Old Man Plymale told me. What do you think? Should I trust him? He seemed to me to be a pretty slippery fellow. And I'm in a profession that has to learn how to spot the unreliable types."

"I think he's a thief. A crook. A totally unscrupulous man," Joanna said. "So why are you working for him? And what is he paying you to do?"

Chandler chuckled. "I think you already know that. He wants me to make sure you don't get the evidence you need to prove you are the direct descendant of Old Man Clarke, thereby recovering for you the estate your father would have inherited, and thereby depriving Mr. Plymale of his ill-gotten charity scam and, much, much worse, thereby subjecting him to a court-ordered audit of what he's done with all that tax-exempt cash. That would probably land him in a federal prison."

Again Chandler waited for a response. Got none.

"It would be a comfy white-collar prison, of course, but he wouldn't like it," he added.

Joanna got up, took a few steps, sat down again, and massaged her leg muscles.

"They say walking downhill, steep ones anyway, is harder on your leg muscles than going up," she said. "Now I believe them."

Chandler nodded. "It's true," he said.

"Why have you been telling me all this? The only reason I can think of is that you want me to cheat Plymale somehow. You want the diamonds."

"Good thinking," Chandler said. "I want to offer you a deal. A partnership. We both hunt the place where this fellow who gave Tuve his diamond lived down here. Little Billy gave me some information to help with the hunt. I have a notion he gave you some, too. Maybe it's the same stuff. How long it took him to go back to his cave, or whatever it was, and come back with the stone. Information like that. But maybe I got some details he forgot to tell you, and you got some he didn't tell me. So my idea is we work together. Improve our chances. Then when we find the cave—and that's what Tuve called it—you find what you want. Your daddy's arm bone with the DNA. Evidence that proves you're his daughter. And we find the diamonds, which we split fifty-fifty."

"Even though they're mine?" Joanna said.

"Insurance company paid for them," Chandler said. "Remember that."

"Paid a hundred thousand dollars."

"But anyway, legally as of now, they belong to the estate, and the estate belongs to that phony charity Plymale controls."

Joanna nodded. Massaging her legs, trying to think of a way she could get into her backpack without making him suspicious. How to get out the pistol.

"I need a drink," she said. If she could reach

around, unzip it, and get out her canteen, maybe she could also slip out the gun. Put it in her jacket pocket. She'd feel safer then. She turned, reached for the backpack.

"Here," Chandler said. "Let me get it for you."

He pulled it off her shoulders, out of her reach, unzipped it, got out the canteen, handed it to her. Got out her pistol, turned it over in his hand, looked at it, checked the chamber and the magazine. Put the muzzle to his nose and sniffed.

"It's still fully loaded," he said. "No burned-powder smell. Is this what you shot Mr. Sherman with?" he asked.

"No," Joanna said, thinking, How could he possibly know about that?

"Well, you won't need it now," he said, and put it in his hip pocket. "And while you're resting a little while, let's compare notes on what Tuve told us. And then we'll go find your bones."

Chandler was laughing now, looking delighted. "And then we'll count out our diamonds and divide 'em up."

21

Bernie Manuelito was still not at the Salt Woman Shrine locale where Sergeant Jim Chee had instructed her to wait. Neither was anyone else. So what was he to do? Chee had not a clue. He had made Cowboy as comfortable as possible for a fellow with a broken and badly swollen leg. He had finally managed to get a call through on his satellite phone to Grand Canyon Park's rescue service and had been assured that either a copter or some other rescue craft would be on hand "as soon as possible."

"You'll just have to wait," Chee told Dashee. "I think I should be going to see if I can find Bernie."

"Good riddance," Dashee said. "It makes me nervous watching you pacing back and forth, biting your fingernails." He groaned, shifted to a more comfortable position on the sand.

"You sure you didn't see any trace of her up around where you were? After all, there's just two ways she could have gone, upriver or downriver, and I didn't see her upriver."

"I am sure," Dashee said. "Absolutely certain. Quit worrying. She'll be back. But you might start worrying about the weather."

Dashee pointed downriver at the towering cumulus cloud, its highest level being blown by stratospheric winds into the flat-topped anvil shape. "That's going to produce what you Navajos call male rains," he said. "Produce lightning, soil erosion, arroyos, floods, and noise. Us Hopis, we like female rains. They produce corn crops and grass. And down here, by the way, you better not let the runoff from one of those catch you in a narrow little canyon."

"I'll worry about the weather, too," Chee said. "But how about if something happened to her?" He pointed at Dashee's ankle. "Something like that. She's smarter than you are, and not so clumsy, but bad things can happen."

"Or how about something even worse happening to you? Like Bernie seeing some nice-looking, polite young tourist guy with one of those float trips coming down the Colorado. She'd realize she could do a lot better than a homely Navajo Tribal Police sergeant with bad manners."

"Bad manners? What do you mean?"

"I'm remembering your tone when you ordered her to wait for you. 'You wait here, Bernie.'" Dashee mimicked Chee's official tone almost exactly.

"Okay," Chee said. "You wait here, Mr. Dashee, and don't hurt yourself again. Have you got enough water?"

"I don't think we'll have to worry about going thirsty for long," Dashee said, and a rumble of thunder punctuated the remark. With that Chee did the only thing he could think of doing: He headed downstream, keeping his eyes and his mind focused on finding the sort of tracks Bernie's little waffle-soled sneakers might have left.

Chee first found Bernie's tracks in the damp sand down by the river. When he couldn't see any more of them there, he headed for any unusual-looking sort of flora along the cliffs and eventually found them again, along with the evidence that Bernie had yielded to her temptation to collect seed pods from whatever plant she considered interesting. His irritation at having to go hunting for her was flooded away by a variety of memories of Bernie—how sweet she looked when deep in thought, when she smiled at him, when she was rapt in admiration of a cloud formation, or a sunset, or the shape of a walnut shell, or the shadows spreading out across the sagebrush slopes when the sun was low. If she was with him now, he thought, she would be admiring the thunderstorm looming above them.

For a while Chee focused on revisiting memories of those times with Bernie, but then the pleasure was interrupted. He began finding other tracks.

Tracks of two people. One wearing hiking boots. Big boots. Size eleven he guessed. The other small, narrow, probably women's casual sportswear. The man was usually walking in front, the woman sometimes stepping on his tracks. The two usually close together. A couple of tourists, he thought, nothing to concern him. Yet they did seem to share Bernie's interest in various growths of canyon-bottom plants.

He sat on a slab of fallen stone at the canyon mouth, taking a sip from his canteen, considering what those tracks meant. A pair of tourists might naturally be curious about the oddity of Grand Canyon botany. Possibly they had no interest in Bernie. Or merely wondered what she was doing.

He recapped his canteen and resumed his tracking, moving a little faster now and enjoying it less, remembering what Lieutenant Leaphorn had so often said about never believing in coincidences.

At the mouth of the next canyon draining into the Colorado, he found Bernie's tracks going in perhaps a hundred yards and the paired tracks following her in and out. Still, he thought, maybe nothing to worry about.

But it did worry him. And he hurried.

Around the next bend in the Colorado's south-side cliff, he came to a wider canyon mouth. Bernie had gone in. The paired tracks had come along after her. Someone wearing small moccasins had also been up this canyon recently. These tracks were faint and Chee spent several minutes seeing what he could learn from them.

Bernie's shoe soles blurred some of them. And some of them, on the way out, had blurred Bernie's tracks. Thus the moccasins had come out after Bernie went in. Interesting but not alarming.

What was alarming was the lack of a sign that either Bernie or the two producing the paired tracks had come out. Chee lost interest in the moccasin tracks and hurried up the side canyon.

The first couple of hundred yards were easy tracking. Both Bernie and the pair following her had walked right up the middle of the smooth stone floor, leaving their prints in the accumulated dust and debris. Then Bernie's disappeared, and it took him a while to discover where she had climbed up a slope where fallen slabs and boulders were piled. Chee climbed it. He found tracks where she had walked around, and the place where she had climbed back down, causing a little avalanche of her own in the process. Under the slope her tracks resumed, as did the paired tracks and multiple traces of the little moccasins.

Bernie's tracks resumed their travels up the canyon floor with the paired tracks following her. But the moccasin tracks didn't.

Why not? Chee had no idea. Nor interest. He cared about Bernie and the big man and little woman so relentlessly trailing her. These three sets of tracks were easy to follow, and Chee followed them at something close to a run. The canyon now boomed with echoing thunder, and the formidable cloud he'd seen before he turned into this side canyon had drifted overhead, darkening his narrow world with its shadow, causing the temperature to drop, and bringing with it a cool breeze.

Chee's running stopped just ahead. On the left side of the canyon was another runoff gorge. It was a narrow slot with its entrance choked by a dense growth of cat's claw acacias—the vegetation detested by cattlemen and sheep herders all across the arid West. The big man's and little woman's shoe prints were there, too, often blurring Bernie's own shoe prints. Bernie was looking for a way in, he guessed, and not finding it.

He paused a moment, thinking, inhaling the suddenly cool, fresh air. A flash of lightning lit the canyon, and just a second behind it came the explosive crack it caused, and the rolling boom of thunder. No time to waste here. He was rushing up the floor of the main canyon, running now because the thunder was becoming almost constant and a shower of popcorn hail had started, the little white balls bouncing off rocks and his hat brim. He had seen her tracks easily until now. But when the real rain started they'd be erased fast.

But there were no more tracks up the canyon. None. No sign of those little waffle soles anywhere, not on the still-dusty smooth stone of the stream bottom, not along the banks, not in any of the places where interesting-looking seed pods might have lured her. Nor were there any signs of the big man's boot prints, which had always been easy to spot.

Which meant what? Bernie hadn't turned back. He wouldn't have missed downhill tracks. She must have found a way through that mass of acacia brush. She must be up in that narrow little slot. And the big man and little woman must be up there with her.

22

When she had first found her way into it, what seemed to her now like hours and hours ago, Bernie had thought of this dark and musty place as a cave. But of course it wasn't. It was a slot, like all of the hundreds of routes rainwater had cut through eons of time in draining runoff from the plateau surfaces a mile above into the Colorado River. Thus its top was open to the sky through a narrow slit. Ahead of her Bernie could see nothing but gloomy semidarkness. But by bending her head back and looking almost straight up, she could see a narrow strip of open sky. It was bright, sunny blue in spots, and obscured by the dark bottoms of clouds in others.

Bernie had clung to this cheerful overhead glimpse of the happy outside world until her neck muscles ached. She urgently yearned to be up there, out there in the clear and bright light and away from here. And she didn't want to look again at what she had just discovered. At least not until her stomach had settled and her heartbeat slowed. But she took a deep, shuddering breath, switched her little flashlight back on, and looked again.

The body she had almost stumbled over was sprawled on a deposit of sand beside the wall of the slot. The base of wall was pink, the color typical of Navajo sandstone. Just above it a shelf of blue-black basalt jutted. On this, a disheveled pile of blankets seemed to have been used as a sort of a bed. Bernie guessed the man had fallen from that bed and rolled down the sloping sand to rest at the edge of the smooth stone floor. Obviously, a long time ago—or at least long enough to cause the dehydrating flesh to shrink and the skin to look like dried leather. He wore neither shoes nor socks, old denim trousers with ragged bottoms, and an unbuttoned long-sleeved denim shirt. His head was turned to the side, revealing just enough of his face to show, before she looked away, the shape of his skull and one empty eye socket.

Bernie sucked in her breath and snapped off the flash. She needed to save her battery. She had to do some exploring. Do it now. Do it fast and get out of here. She had to find Jim Chee and Cowboy Dashee. Tell them about this. That she had found the man who had given Tuve the diamond. Probably this was the man they had been looking for. Anyway, she had found some sort of hermit. At least something that seemed very strange.

Bernie leaned against the cold stone of the wall, recognizing how shaky her legs were, how exhausted she'd become. And she still had, as Robert Frost had put it, promises to keep and miles to go before she'd sleep.

Miles to go back to the Salt Trail, and then miles to bring Chee and Dashee back here. They'd never find the way in here—through that dreadful tangle of cat's claw acacia brush—without her showing them. She'd almost given up herself, after snagging herself a half-dozen times on those awful thorns.

The acacias had closed over the bed of the runoff stream that ran—whenever a rainstorm produced some drainage—out of the slot. It had finally occurred to Bernie that the heat from those sun-facing slot walls would discourage the acacias right against the cliff. There she had managed to slip through with only a torn sleeve.

And while doing it she had noticed the old pruning that someone had done years ago to keep that narrow path open. That seemed to prove that someone had once occupied this slot, whether or not it was Billy Tuve's dispenser of diamonds.

When she snapped on the light again and turned it up the slot, what she saw seemed to make that certain. In the gloom ahead the flashlight beam touched off an odd glittering.

Bernie walked slowly toward it. Two vertical lines, perhaps two feet apart and maybe four feet high, flashed back at the flashlight beam. They were arranged on a basalt shelf, probably an extension of the one holding the blankets. But since the slot floor slanted upward, here the shelf was only about knee high over floor level. The glittering spots of light seemed to be coming from the sandstone wall above the basalt level. Now that she was close, she could see that something stood between the lines of flashing dots. It looked like a white bone.

She stepped closer, stopped and stared. It was a human arm bone. Elbow to wrist, with the bones of the hand still attached by tendons and gristle. Before she had resigned her job with the Navajo Tribal Police, Bernie had spent a few unpleasant duty hours in morgue and autopsy rooms. That had partly accustomed her to dismembered human body parts. But not totally, and the setting here made it worse than usual.

Strange indeed. The spots of glittering light were coming from little round tins that seemed to be attached somehow to the sandstone. She counted twenty such tins in each row, each containing a diamond, which glittered in the light. The forearm bone was still connected at the elbow to the upper arm bone, most of that buried under packed sand. On the sand around it, neat circles of diamonds were arrayed, each perched on a little grayish pad of leather in a small round tin.

Bernie reached for one, hesitated, then picked it up. The pad was formed of the soft folded leather of a pollen pouch. The container was a tin can that, according to the faded red legend on its side, once contained **Truly Sweet**. A smaller line below that declared that to be "The World's Mildest Dipping Snuff." That was exactly the way Lieutenant Leaphorn had described the container that had held the Shorty McGinnis diamond.

She unfolded the pouch, put the diamond in

it, stuck it back in the snuff can, and put it in the pocket of her jeans.

Bernie was feeling exuberant. Now she would get out of this dismal place. She would go find Jim and Cowboy. She'd tell them the mission was complete. She had found the diamonds and the body of the dispenser of diamonds. She had found the evidence that would clear poor Billy Tuve of the murder charge. And the robbery charge. And any doubts that Sergeant Jim Chee might have entertained about Officer Bernadette Manuelito would be forever erased.

She started down the smooth stone floor of the slot, pausing here and there to inspect a rock shelf where the hermit had stored his food supplies in cans and sacks and his drinking water in five-gallon tins. Nearby she located his water source, a dripping, moss-grown trickle originating from a spring back in a crack in the slot wall. She let it drip into her palm and cautiously tasted it. It didn't seem poisonous. Probably hadn't run through any rock layers contaminated by chemicals and metallic ores.

She turned off her flashlight. The light reflecting through the slot above was dimmer now, but there was still enough reflected to guide her.

It was getting close to sundown, though, and she hurried down the slanting floor to get to the mouth of this slot, and back down the canyon to the Colorado River, while she still had some daylight. It was then that she heard a woman's voice, coming from down the slot, echoing as every sound did in this otherwise silent place. And then a man's voice—close enough so she could understand it. The man said, "Ms. Craig. Keep your voice down. Let's keep it very quiet. She might be dangerous."

23

"I wasn't raising my voice," Joanna Craig said, in something close to an indignant whisper. "And why dangerous? It's either a smallish woman or a tiny little man," she said. "Judging from the size of their shoes."

Brad Chandler didn't respond to that. Instead he put his finger to his lips, put a hand behind an ear, signaling to Joanna that they should listen. She did, and heard nothing but the tinkling sound of water dripping from the gloomy passageway far ahead up the slot and the occasional faint sigh of the wind blowing past the slot's open roof far overhead.

"We'll go in a little farther," Chandler whispered. "If all remains quiet and we see no sign of anyone, then I'll give us a little better light. We want to pick up that woman's track again. She must have some reason for being in here."

"Sure," Joanna said.

"And you have to take for granted it's dangerous. There's a lot of money involved in this, and where there's money, there are dangerous people."

"Okay," Joanna said. "I understand."

He made a sort of chuckling sound. "And maybe she's a little woman, but you're not so big yourself. And even little women can be packing pistols. Remember?"

"I remember you forgot to return mine," Joanna said. "If it's dangerous in here, I'd feel a lot safer with it. Didn't you say we're partners?"

"Right," Chandler said. "But don't let it worry you. I always look after my partners."

He snapped on his heavy police-model flashlight, directing its beam back and forth across the smooth stone floor.

"There," Joanna said, pointing. On the dusty stone were the faint tracks left by Bernie's waffle soles.

As far as the light reached through the gloom, the tracks seemed to continue in an irregular line along the right edge of the floor.

"Let's hope it stays this easy," Chandler said.

"Take a look up," Joanna said. "At the sky almost straight overhead."

Chandler glanced at Joanna, suspicious.

"I saw a flash of lightning," she said.

A boom of thunder punctuated her statement, producing a deafening battery of echoes from the cliffs.

"Guess it's going to rain," Chandler said, looking up now. "We'll be dry in here. And if it keeps doing that, you can talk as loud as you like."

"Yes," she began, intending to tell this big, obnoxious man what she had read about the effects of rainstorms above the canyon. And what one of the people at the Park Service Center had told her of the sudden flash floods roaring down the little washes that drained the mesa tops. But no. Maybe that knowledge, and his ignorance, might be useful if she had any luck. And Joanna Craig had no doubt that she was going to need a lot of luck to get out of this situation.

He shifted the light beam, revealing nothing but the uneven layers of stone of the slot cliffs to the left, then he directed it up the cliffs, then across the slot. The light produced a brief burst of glitter as it passed the diamonds and then illuminated the cliffs to the right.

"There!" Chandler said, keeping the beam focused on the high shelf where Bernie had seen the diamond man's bed. "See the cloth? I think we've found something."

"Didn't you notice something shining?" Joanna asked. She pointed. "Back that way."

Chandler ignored her. Walked toward the shelf.

"Somebody had a bed roll up there," he said. "This must be where the man with the diamonds lived."

And as he said that, the beam of the flash struck the corpse.

Joanna sucked in her breath.

"Yes," Chandler said. "I see him now. Or what's left of him."

He focused the light on the body. "Looks like somebody got here first," he said, and switched the flashlight into his left hand and used his right to take out his pistol.

"You're not going to need that gun," Joanna said. "He's already dead. A long time dead, the way he looks."

"I can see that, dammit," Chandler said. "But who killed him?"

"Look at him," Joanna said. "Maybe it was

time. Old age. Anyway, it certainly wasn't very recently. He's practically a mummy."

"I see it now," Chandler said. "And look, here's some more of those footprints. All around here. She's probably close. Anyway, I'll keep this pistol handy." He shined the light directly into Joanna's face. "Might need it," he said, grinning at her.

Joanna turned away from the flashlight, held out her hand. "Then give me mine. Maybe I'll need it."

He ignored that, swinging the flashlight beam past the body.

"And there," he said. "Wow. Just look at that. Those must be my diamonds."

"Arranged in two rows," Joanna said. But she was staring at the white shape standing between the glittering columns. And thinking, My father's arm. And noticing this man had said "my diamonds." Not that she had ever believed he would share them with her. Or that she cared about the diamonds anyway, for that matter. The bone was what she wanted.

24

Bernie had reacted fast at the first sound of the voices. Strange voices. The man's voice had an East Coast urban sound. Not Jim and not Cowboy, and it certainly didn't sound like what she'd expect Billy Tuve to sound like. Who were they? What were they doing here? And why were they following her?

Lieutenant Leaphorn believed these diamonds were involved in a legal battle so big it had attracted FBI interest. Both of these people were armed. Park Service rules prohibited firearms in the canyon, so they weren't merely tourists. If they thought she was dangerous to them, they might be dangerous to her. She ran up the slanting floor as fast and as quietly as the rock-cluttered pathway allowed. She wanted to find a place as far from the voices as she could get. A place where she could conceal herself until she could locate a way out of this slot.

Instead she ran almost immediately into a dead end. Part of one of the cliff walls had collapsed into a towering dam of chunks, slabs, and boulders blocking the floor and partially the slot. She climbed. A chunk of sandstone slid under her weight and dislodged smaller stones, bruising Bernie's knee and starting a rattling little landslide that touched off a chorus of echoes. Surely they would have heard that. She moved cautiously toward the wall, slid under a tilted slab leaning against it, and sat down.

Time to subdue panic. Time to rest. Time to think. Time to make a plan.

Thinking came first. Remembering everything she had heard from Chee about the genesis of this crazy business. Then remembering (now she could hardly believe this) her voluntarily tagging along uninvited and unwanted.

Why? Out of a sense of adventure? Out of a yen to get a close look at the botanical/geological magic of this incredible canyon? Well, that was her excuse and it was partly true. But mostly it was to be with Jim Chee. She loved Jim Chee. Or thought she did. But where was Sergeant Chee now, when she really needed him?

Bernie slid a little deeper under the slab, trying to get more comfortable, realizing this line of thought was utterly unproductive. She had to remember what else she knew, things that might tell her something about this couple she was hiding from. Everything she knew about that might bear on what she must do now. Just what Chee had heard from Lieutenant Leaphorn, who had harvested it from his lifelong and nationwide Cop Good Old Boy Network.

The FBI was interested in a Gallup pawnshop arrest, which had to mean somebody big in the Washington bureaucracy was interested, which according to the inter-cop psychic vibration connected it to an old legal battle over a plutocrat's estate, the outcome of which had left a nonprofit foundation with the money and a woman who thought she should have inherited it determined to get it back. A great pile of money was involved and—as she had overheard the man telling the woman—you have to connect piles of money with dangerous people trying to get it.

Probably true in the white man's world, Bernie thought, and in this canyon, too. Both of them had arrived with guns, which made them fit Bernie's notion of dangerous people. And now the man had the woman's gun, and the woman wanted it back, and he wouldn't give it to her. That, and the tone of the conversation, suggested they were not really partners in whatever they were doing here. She guessed the woman was the one who thought she had been cheated out of her inheritance. The one who had put up the money to bail Tuve out of jail. Because he had one of the diamonds. If she remembered what she'd heard from Chee, this woman believed the man carrying the case of diamonds was her father and that the foundation's lawyer had cheated her out of her inheritance.

Bernie groaned. Not enough data to figure out anything useful in this situation. Wishing she had really paid attention to what Chee had been saying. At the time it had seemed like another fairy tale. Sort of like the Havasupai version of how a shaman had forced the Grand Canyon cliffs to stop clapping themselves together to kill people by walking across the river with a tree log on his head.

The man? Was he someone she had brought along to help her until their deal went sour? Or maybe someone representing the foundation, here to protect its interests?

Bernie had no way to decide that, but she knew that if she stayed half hidden here, they would find her if they wanted to. She had to have a plan.

A flash of lightning erased the gloom down the slot below where she sat, giving her a momentary glimpse of the place the diamond dispenser had lived and died, and of a small woman and a big man standing near it. The following crash of thunder started echoes bouncing around the slot. Another flash illuminated the scene. The man, she now saw, was holding a white stick in his hand, waving it. Probably the arm bone of the skeleton man.

She had to stop wasting time. She had to have a plan.

25

"Put it down," Joanna Craig said.

Chandler laughed. "I'm just enjoying the thought of walking up to Mr. Plymale and waving this in the old bastard's face," he said. "I'd say, 'Okay, you old bastard, here it is. How much will you offer me for it?'"

"Give it to me," Joanna said. "It's mine. It's my father's arm."

"Possession is nine-tenths of the law," Chandler said. "So let's talk business. You can take custody of your daddy's bone. I'll take the diamonds."

Joanna nodded.

"I mean all the diamonds. Each and every one."

"I don't care about the damned diamonds," Joanna said. "Give me my father's bone."

Chandler stared at her. Looked thoughtful. Nodded.

"Why not?" he said. "But how about that woman we followed in here. She must have known about this place. I'm sort of uneasy about her. I want you to go on up there and see if you can find her."

Joanna considered this, held out her hand.

"Okay," she said. "You said she was dangerous. Give me my pistol."

Chandler laughed. "If you have that pistol, then you might be dangerous. I don't think you'll need it, anyway. Those little footprints said either a little woman or a small boy. Right? And the Park Service doesn't allow people to carry guns down here."

He got out his own pistol, grinned, pointed it at Joanna.

"Get along now. Find that woman and bring her down here." He looked at his watch. "I'll give you ten minutes and then I'll come after you."

Joanna started up the sloping floor. Stopped. Turned to look back at Chandler.

"What now?" Chandler said. "Get going."

Joanna pointed at a figure walking down the

slope toward her out of the gloom. "This must be her," she said.

Chandler swung his flashlight around. "How about that," he said. "I guess we have company."

26

The flashlight blinded Bernie.

"Turn it off," she said, snapping on her own flashlight. "Turn it off." She shaded her eyes, turned her own light on Chandler.

"I said **turn it off now**."

Chandler lowered the light. "Who are you?" he asked.

"What are you people doing in here?" Bernie asked. "And did I hear something about a pistol? This is a National Park with no firearms permitted. If you have one, hand it over."

Joanna nodded toward Chandler, said, "He has—" Then stopped.

"And I'll need to see your visitors' permits," Bernie said. "The form they gave you when you checked in and got permission to come down here without an authorized Park Service guide."

Chandler had been studying Bernie, motion-less and wordless. Now he shook his head, laughed. "I'll have to see your credentials."

"First I'll take the pistol," Bernie said. "I heard this lady say you had it."

"You don't look like a Park Service ranger to me," Chandler said. "Where's the uniform? Where's the official Park Service shoulder patch? All I see is a little woman in dusty blue jeans and a torn shirt and one of those New York Giants ball caps."

"Turn over the pistol," Bernie said. "Just hav-ing a firearm down here is a federal offense. You add a citation of refusing to obey a federal offi-cer to that charge, and you're going to be facing a federal felony indictment."

"Oh well," Chandler said. "Why argue about it."

He extracted a pistol from a jacket pocket, extended it toward Bernie, muzzle forward. And not, she noticed, extended far enough so she could take it without getting within his easy reach. It looked like one of the Glock automatic models used by a lot of police forces.

"Turn it around butt first and toss it to me," Bernie ordered.

"All right," Chandler said.

He raised the pistol, pointed it at Bernie.

"Now," he said, "let's quit wasting time. Get out your Park Service credentials and show me. Or your badge, or whatever you carry. And if you've got a gun on you, which I don't see, we'll want that, too."

"I don't have my badge with me. This is an undercover assignment. We're checking into a report we've had."

"Oh, really!" Chandler said.

"My partner will be in here anytime joining me. If he sees you holding that gun on me, he'll shoot first and then ask what you're doing. Better give it to me."

"Put your arms straight out from your sides," he said. "Miss Craig here is going to pat you down. See if you have a weapon. You would have, even if you are doing something undercover."

"You're getting into serious trouble. Both of you."

"Go pat her down," Chandler said, nodding to Joanna. "Make sure she doesn't have a weapon."

"No. No," Joanna said. "I'm not having anything to do with this."

Chandler stared at her, expression grim.

"I see," he said. Then, to Bernie: "Turn

around, little lady, arms straight out, hands open." He took a step forward, checked for a shoulder holster, checked her belt line, patted her on the back. Nodded.

"Now that that's out of the way, I'll show you my credentials." He took out his billfold, opened it, thrust it at Bernie's face. "There you see my own badge as a Los Angeles County, California, deputy sheriff. And here"—he took a card from his billfold—"is my authorization as a criminal investigator for the same county. I am here to continue an investigation of a cold case, an old homicide in California, the investigation of which has led us all the way out here."

Bernie nodded, very aware that Chandler had jerked both the badge and the certification card away before she had a chance to read them. The man was lying, but perhaps he was a private investigator with some sort of credentials. The world seemed to be full of them.

The thunder was booming again. The sharp crack of a lightning strike on the mesa top near the slot echoed around them. Bernie noticed the dusty stone streambed was no longer dusty. It was carrying a thin sheet of water. And as she watched, it repeated something she'd seen untold times after the "male rains" of summer in desert mesa country—another wave of runoff raced down the floor and left the thin sheet an inch or so deeper. She felt a sense of urgency. Another such wave would be coming, and another, and another. As gravity rushed the runoff water down, the stream would become a flood.

"Well, then," she said, "what can I do to assist you?"

"Just take a seat somewhere and stay out of the way," Chandler said. "We want to get our evidence collected and get out of here before this storm turns into something serious."

He picked up the strap of his backpack, pulled it away from the stream floor, and zipped it open. Bernie watched as he sorted through its contents, moving a shirt out of the way, pushing aside underwear, shoving a small pistol under the shirt, finally taking out a pair of heavy wool socks. He inspected them and looked at his companion.

"Joanna," he said. "You got any sort of sack in your pack?"

"For what?" she said.

"For what we came for," he said, and pointed to the double line of diamonds.

She shook her head.

"Hell with it, then," Chandler said. He tucked one of the socks under his belt, went to the shelf where the bone had been erected, and began picking snuff tins off the sand there, dropping the diamonds into the other sock and tossing aside the empty containers. It took longer than it might have because he was keeping his pistol ready.

Diamond after diamond clicked into the sock. Bernie watched and counted, conscious of the time, aware that the runoff stream was widening fast, thinking of how much water that dam of fallen stones up the slot must be holding back. What was flowing past now was merely what was running under the slab where she had been sitting. If it came over the dam, if the dam washed out, everything here would be swept down the slot canyon.

Chandler stopped. All the tins on the sand were emptied now and the foot of the sock, from heel to toe, bulged with diamonds. He tucked the pistol in his belt, knotted the sock at the ankle, and began extracting diamonds from the tins fastened to the sandstone wall, dropping them into the second sock, knotting it above the diamonds, tying the two socks into a single strand with each end a bulging knot of diamonds.

Job done, he faced the women.

"Here we have a big bunch of diamonds," he said, gripping the combined socks where they were knotted, and swinging the bulges back and forth and laughing. "Big diamonds. Perfect blue-whites with expensive cuts. About thirty or so in this sock and"—he pointed—"maybe forty or so in this one. Call it seventy, and multiply that by maybe twenty thousand dollars on the average, and I have let's say a million and a half dollars."

Thunder drowned out what else Chandler was telling them. The storm now must have moved directly overhead. Water was dripping down from the rim of the slot above. The light popcorn hail was peppering directly on them now. The flow down the slot floor was widening fast.

Bernie made a "wait" gesture to Chandler with an open palm, rushed to his backpack, and pulled it away from the spreading water. She reached under the shirt, extracted Joanna's little pistol, slipped it into her pocket, zipped the pack shut, picked it up, and deposited it on high ground well away from the flood. Then she exhaled. The man hadn't noticed, so he hadn't shot her. Not yet. She glanced at him. He was grinning at her.

"Thanks," he said.

"It would have washed away," she said. "There's sort of a dam up there where rocks fell down. If the runoff sweeps that out, everything is going to wash away. We better get out of here."

"Nice of you to warn me," Chandler said. "And thank you for saving Joanna's little pistol from getting wet."

"Oh," Bernie said.

"In return for your kindness, I guess I should tell you that when you get a chance to shoot me, and try to do it, just don't try. It won't work. I unloaded Joanna's pistol, just in case she got careless with it."

He laughed. "However, if you try to shoot me anyway, then I want you to know that I will shoot you. Probably several times. And"—he pointed to the shriveled body of the Skeleton Man— "leave your body here with our deceased friend."

"Thanks for the warning," Bernie said.

While she was saying it, lightning flashed again, followed a moment later by the crack of a nearby strike, and booming echoes of thunder. And as that faded, another sound emerged.

"Ooooh!" said Joanna, in something between a shout and a shriek. It was a rumbling, creaking, crashing sound of boulders being swept along by the overpowering surge of flash waters rushing down-slope. With the sound came the sight of the slot-bottom stream abruptly rising, spreading, sweeping along with it the variety of leaves, twigs, assorted debris the bottom had collected in the years since the last "male rain" downpour had settled over this section of the Coconino Plateau and sent untold tons of water pouring off the rocky surface into the canyon.

Bernie had expected this, but in a more gradual and less violent form, and had decided what she had to do when it happened.

Chandler had not waited for a plan to reveal itself. He was running down the slot, splashing along the edge of the stream against the cliff. Looking for a place to climb, she guessed, or hoping to reach the exit where the slot would pour its water into the canyon. He was clutching his diamond-filled socks as he ran.

Bernie grabbed Joanna Craig's arm. "Come on!" she shouted. "I know a place we'll be safe."

Saying it, Bernie was wishing she felt as confident as she tried to sound. The place she had in mind was the basalt shelf where the Skeleton Man had made his bed. He must have known the canyon, perched there to be safe from such flash floods. And coming in here, she had noticed on the walls of the slot how high flood debris had been deposited by previous floods. Maybe the Skeleton Man's shelf wasn't totally safe, but it would be safer than here.

And Joanna Craig seemed to trust her. She was following, splashing along with the rushing water. Knee-deep now, it was pushing them along, hurrying them, trying to sweep their feet off the bottom. And then they were at the edge of the sloping shelf.

Bernie pulled herself onto it, feeling as she did the water sweeping her feet out of its way, helping Joanna pull herself up, then helping her hoist the man's bright yellow backpack up with her.

They sat for a moment, regaining their breath.

"Why did you save that?" Bernie asked, tapping the wet backpack.

Joanna Craig unzipped it, reached in, extracted the arm bone, showed it to Bernie. Smiling.

"This is what I came here for," she said, and Bernie could tell she was crying. "Now I can prove I'm my father's daughter."

27

The first time he had been to the bottom of the Grand Canyon, Jim Chee had thought of the Colorado River system as a sort of reverse copy of a human vascular arrangement, with the Colorado being the artery and the scores of smaller canyons leading down into it the capillaries. Gravity made it all work backward, of course. The little gullies and arroyos collected water from all over the Kaibab and Coconino plateaus to feed their area streams across the immense Colorado Plateau. Then these creeks and rivers poured it down into the Colorado a mile or more below. Having seen the velocity that gravity gave the torrents coming off the lava mesas in northern New Mexico, he guessed he'd find runoff into the Grand Canyon (with ten times more gravity behind it) absolutely spectacular.

He was right.

Chee was huddled into a modest overhang at the cliff where the canyon he'd followed from the big river was joined by runoff pouring out of a small slot. He was wet to the skin from the pounding rain—mixed now and then with bits of hail. He was also scratched and bruised from a futile attempt to buck the runoff from the smaller stream. The racing water had knocked him out of the way and deposited him, half drowned, beside the cliff where he now stood. And that stream was puny compared to the roaring runoff it was joining.

He was as certain as the situation allowed that the slot he'd tried to enter was the one into which Bernie had disappeared. She and whoever she was with must be in that slot now. Maybe they were already drowning. If they drowned, they would wash out here. He had already seen part of a wooden bucket flash by on the flood.

Now came what looked like some sort of cloth and what might have been a soggy hat. Behind that, bobbing and turning, came what seemed to be a dried and terribly emaciated corpse. It was clad in a torn blue shirt and ragged denim pants. The hair plastered to the skull was white and the body was so wasted that the bones pressed against the skin. The torrent quickly swept it past to disappear in the foam where the stream pouring out of the slot joined the much larger main canyon flood.

"Skeleton Man," Chee said. Well, they had finally found him. Or Bernie had found him. And all he could do about her being up there in the slot, and in danger, was wait and worry until the flood subsided.

The water pouring out of the slot, and the flood racing down the canyon, produced a roaring bedlam made even more deafening by the echoes bouncing off the cliffs. But suddenly Chee heard what seemed to be a yell. Brief, and suddenly choked off.

A moment later a man shot out of the slot, head out of the water, trying to swim.

Chee jumped to his feet, scrambled away from the wall and down the slope toward the flood.

The man grabbed at the branches of cat's claw acacia he was being swept past, managed to catch a branch, held on. The force of the water swept his legs downstream. He was on his back now, seeing Chee.

"Help!" he screamed. "Help me!"

"Coming," Chee shouted. "Hold on."

The man was holding on only with his left hand, clutching what seemed to be a sort of rope in the other.

"Use both hands!" Chee yelled. "I'll wade in as far as I can. When I get close enough, you push off and I'll try to catch you."

The man looked at Chee, expression desperate, tried to say something, couldn't. Then he swung his right arm, trying for a hold on another limb. The rope he was holding swung upward, caught in the brambles. The man grabbed at it.

Trying to pull himself up, Chee thought. Impossible. The brush wouldn't hold his weight. Chee took another step into the water, almost to his knees now, struggling to keep a foothold on the rock below, leaning against the pressure of the water.

The man was frantically jerking at the rope.

"For God's sake, don't jerk it loose," Chee told him. "Just get yourself braced and push off and try to swim toward me. Hey, stop jerking!"

The rope tore free, bringing a piece of cat's claw limb with it. The man went under, bobbed up, turned sideways to the force of the flow. It swept him past Chee's hands, beyond any hope of Chee's reaching him.

Chee staggered back into shallow water, turned to look.

The torrent was rolling the man now. He disappeared under it for a second or two, then bobbed up with his hand still clutching the rope. Then the torrent from the slot reached the flood roaring down the canyon. In the foam and confusion, the man disappeared.

Chee leaned against the cliff, regaining his breath. No sign of the man now. He imagined what would be happening to him. The big flood in the canyon was rolling boulders along with it. He could hear the crashing and banging they produced as they knocked away impediments. He might be floating high enough to escape that kind of death. At least for a while. Chee remembered the big dropoff a mile or so down the canyon. That would be a violent waterfall by now. The current would sweep the man to its bottom there, churn him around with those rolling boulders, and spit out what was left of him to continue the trip down to the next waterfall, and the next one, and through the various rapids, and on to the canyon's confluence with the Colorado. Unless some rafters saw what was left of him caught in the flotsam at the foot of a rapids somewhere, he'd make it all the way down to Boulder Dam.

But the rain had almost finished drenching this part of the Grand Canyon and was drifting northeastward, leaving the Coconino Plateau to dump its tons of water across the Colorado on the Kaibab Plateau. Now the canyons draining the other rim of the great river would be roaring with flood.

Chee took a hard look at the torrent pouring out of the slot. In a few minutes he could buck it. In a few hours it would be a mere trickle. In a few days the stone floor of the slot would be dry again, collecting dust, waiting for the next male rain to flush it clean.

Ten minutes later, Chee was splashing wearily upstream against the diminishing flow. Calling for Bernie.

28

"I think it would be safe enough," Bernie said. "The water's not so deep now. Not running so fast. Let's climb down and get out of here."

Joanna Craig looked doubtful. "How about that man?" she asked. "He's down there somewhere. And he has his pistol."

"I think he's gone," Bernie said. "Gone forever. And we have your pistol, too."

"I don't know, though. What if he comes back?"

"If he comes back, we shoot him," Bernie said. "Let's get out of here before there's more rain and it gets worse again."

"He said he unloaded the pistol."

"He said it, but he didn't do it. I checked. It's still loaded."

"Do you know how to shoot it?"

"I'm a policewoman," Bernie said, and was surprised to hear the pride in her voice. Noticing she hadn't said "former policewoman." She'd thought she'd gotten over that.

They eased their way down off the platform into the water flow. Not much more than ankle-deep now, but cold. No matter how hot the summer day, these male rains in the high country were always icy. If Jim was here to hear her, she'd be tempted to say "cold as a police sergeant's heart."

Even as she thought that, she heard his voice, and her name. The echoes off the slot's cliffs were repeating it: "Bernie, Bernie, Bern, Ber . . ." But even in the echoes she recognized Jim's voice.

"Jim!" she shouted. "We're up here. We're coming down the wash."

That, too, immediately translated itself into a clamor of echoes. But he would have understood enough of it.

"Come on," Bernie said, leading Joanna on a splashing run down the stream. With Bernie thinking she didn't really know whether the blond man with the gun was actually gone forever. Thinking she should have warned Jim. Thinking it was too late for that now. Stopping to get Joanna's pistol out of her pocket, just in case.

And when they started running again there was Jim Chee, splashing toward them.

"Bernie!" he shouted, still running. "Thank God."

"Jim," she said, gesturing toward Joanna, "this is Joanna Craig and—"

Their reunion was too violent for that sentence to be completed. He splashed into Bernie, partly due to enthusiasm, partly because he had lost his balance. The impact of a soggy man with a fairly dry woman was forceful enough to send out a spray. Then they were hugging each other with force and enthusiasm.

"Jim," Bernie said, when she had recovered enough breath to say it. "Where have you been? I was afraid you—"

"I thought I had lost you, Bernie," Chee blurted out. And, alas, added: "Why didn't you wait for me? I thought I told you—" He was smart enough to end it there.

Bernie backed away a little. "Ms. Craig," she said, "this is Sergeant Jim Chee of the Navajo

Tribal Police. He used to be my boss. Sometimes he thinks he still is."

"How do you do," Chee said to Joanna. "And we're going to be married right away," and he hugged Bernie again.

Bernie found herself talking directly into his left ear. "Jim, there's a man in here. With a pistol. Claims to be a deputy from California. Big blond man."

"He's gone," Chee said, still hugging Bernie. "Washed down the canyon out there, and on down into the Colorado."

"It's good to meet you, Mr. Chee," Joanna said. "But if it's safe now, we should get out of this water. Get someplace out in the open air."

They started down the runoff flow, which was diminishing quickly, with Bernie talking fast about how she had gotten here, about the diamonds, about the arrival of Joanna and Chandler, about the dried, emaciated corpse, about Chandler taking the diamonds.

"That body washed by me," Chee said. "And so did the blond man, carrying some sort of rope knotted on the ends. In fact, I think I might have been able to save him, but the rope got caught in that cat's claw brush at the mouth of this slot. Instead of trying to get to where I could pull him to the bank, he was trying to jerk it loose."

"That rope had all those diamonds in it," Bernie said, and explained how Chandler had rigged two long wool hiker's socks together to carry them.

"Well, they're gone now," Chee said. "Maybe they'll sink to the bottom of the Colorado River, or wash all the way down to Lake Mead."

"They were Ms. Craig's diamonds," Bernie said. "Or would have been. I saved one of them for Billy Tuve to use as evidence—if he needs it."

She took the snuff can from her pocket, handed it to Chee. "Be careful, Jim. Don't you drop it."

Chee grinned at her. "Now, Bernie, you're not supposed to talk to me like that until after I'm your husband."

But he was careful with it, taking out the folder pouch, putting diamond in pouch, pouch in can, and can in his pocket.

The early twilight of the world outside the slot greeted them now. They ducked under the cat's claw brush and walked out of the now-shallow flow to the cliff-side bank where Chee had waited.

"Free at last," Bernie said, and they began their trek down the canyon to its confluence with the Colorado. The big canyon flow was also sharply diminished now. Chee finished his account of Dashee's misfortune just as they reached the big river. There they heard a helicopter over the rim.

"That will be the one coming for Dashee," Chee said. "I hope he's smart enough to get them to wait a little while in case we show up."

He was. On the flight back to the Park Service landing pad, Chee presented Dashee with the snuff can, pouch, and diamond, Billy Tuve's evidence to get the charges against him dismissed.

"And don't forget to tell Tuve to get the diamond he actually owns out of the court's evidence room," Chee said. "And after he uses the one Bernie salvaged from the Skeleton Man shrine as evidence to get his charge dropped, tell the sheriff to start looking for another suspect in that Zuni homicide, and then I guess he should give that diamond to Miss Craig, here."

"Or maybe the insurance company will claim

it," Joanna said. "I'll get my attorney, to decide how to handle that."

"One more thing," Chee said. "Tell Tuve not to try to pawn that twenty-thousand-buck diamond of his for twenty dollars again. It makes pawnshops suspicious."

"And causes way too much trouble," Bernie said.

"Well, I can think of one good thing that came out of all this," Chee said. "Old Joe Leaphorn's been retired long enough so those tales he likes to tell at those little Navajo Inn coffee meetings are getting awful stale. When he hears all the details, this one's going to give him ammunition for another couple of years."

At Park Service headquarters the party broke up. After much handshaking and good-byes, Joanna went off to the Grand Hotel for a hot bath and a long sleep. Cowboy was hauled away to the hospital for an ankle x-ray and a cast. And Chee arranged for a ride for Bernie and himself back to where his car was parked near the Salt Trail terminus on the Grand Canyon rim.

Total exhaustion won its battle over Bernie's postadventure excitement very early on her drive homeward with Chee, but not before some loose ends had been dealt with. Chee had told her that if she was willing, he would pick her up tomorrow and they could scout for a house to buy, or a building lot if that seemed a better idea.

"You know, Jim," said Bernie, "I went back to your mobile-home place yesterday—or was it the day before yesterday, I'm too tired to remember—and I think you're right. I think we should live there at first. Then if we don't like it, we can do something else."

"I can't believe I'm hearing this," Chee said.

"Well, I went by there and you weren't home, so I walked around it. Sort of inspected. And it could be fixed up some."

"You're just saying this because you're tired, and damp, and so sleepy you can hardly keep your eyes open. You just don't feel up to renewing our old argument."

Bernie laughed, sort of feebly. "No. It's because I sat there on that log you like to sit on, and I watched the river go by, and the breeze blowing in the cottonwoods, and listened to all the birds that hang around there. And I just felt comfortable with it."

"Well, how about that," Chee said. And that was followed by a period of meditation.

"Bernie, I was just going to tell you that I've

had a big 'For Sale' sign painted. Already have it put up on the highway, with an arrow pointing toward my place. And I called in a want ad to the advertising people at the **Gallup Independent** and the **Farmington Times,** giving my telephone number and—"

Bernie broke the Navajo "don't interrupt" code.

"How did you describe it?"

"Well, I said, 'Beautiful shady site overlooking San Juan River on the west edge of Shiprock with roomy, attractive, and comfortable mobile home trailer. Electric and phone lines installed.'"

Bernie laughed and reached over and hugged him.

"You didn't mention water."

"Well, it's no big deal to haul your water in. There's that storage tank there by the trailer, and the hose runs into the kitchen, and—"

"Another hose into the bathroom. Right?"

"Well, I didn't mention the bathroom problem."

Bernie didn't answer that.

"I thought about trying to explain that arrangement, but they charge by the word. And I was afraid that might sort of, you know, diminish the appeal. What do you think?"

"I think it would diminish the appeal," Bernie said, and yawned.

"I'll try to work out a brief way to put it," Chee said. "Do you have any suggestions?"

But, alas, Bernie was already asleep.

29

Captain Pinto returned to the table the Navajo Inn diner had come to reserve for Leaphorn and friends' coffee chats. He carried a tray of doughnuts, one for each participant. He took the chocolate one for himself, said, "Pick the one you like," and sat down.

"Joe," he said. "You were going to tell us how that slow-moving love affair between Sergeant Chee and Bernie Manuelito came out of this. Did I miss anything?"

"Nothing interesting," Captain Largo said.

"Well, I think you all know the happy ending," Leaphorn said. "They had a fine traditional wedding at her mother's place. But . . ."

"But what?" Pinto asked.

"Well, apparently Chee's performance down in the canyon made such an impression on

Bernie that she gave in, and they're living in that little old house trailer Jim calls home."

"I'll bet that won't last long," Largo said. "That Manuelito girl, she's something else."

They tried their doughnuts, sipped coffee.

"Bernie heard from that Joanna Craig woman," Leaphorn announced. "The one who was trying to recover her daddy's arm bone. She said they've done the DNA test, and they have a perfect match. She told Bernie the lawyer who got control of the estate involved in this, he called her lawyer and was offering some sort of deal. And Joanna said she'd rather burn in hell than make a deal with that man."

"Another thing," Pinto said. "I heard Tuve told the Arizona State Police that Ms. Craig shot that private eye, that Sherman. How'd she get out of that?"

"The way I heard it, Sherman was maybe a little embarrassed getting shot by a woman with his own pistol, or maybe it was he didn't want a lot of digging into what he was doing out there. Anyway, he insisted that it was an accident. Claimed he was fooling with the pistol and it went off."

"What's that all about?" said Largo. "I wasn't in on that."

"Don't ask," Pinto said. "It's way too complicated to understand."

"Well, how about the diamonds, then?" Largo said.

"Chee told me the Park Service and the Arizona people recovered the body of that Chandler fella. The Colorado River had washed him all the way down to the shallow end of Lake Mead. But no diamonds on him. Found the body of the Skeleton Man, too. But no identification. No more chance of doing that than they have of finding the diamonds."

Joe Leaphorn, the legendary lieutenant, was smiling. "Just think. Million of dollars' worth of diamonds on the riverbottom. Or Lake Mead. Maybe the pumps will suck some of them up. Maybe we'll be hearing of diamonds being sprayed out of those wonderful Las Vegas fountains. Just think of the new set of legends this is going to produce."